MAROONED WITH THE MILLIONAIRE

NINA MILNE

MILLS & BOON

First published in Great Britain 2018
by Mills & Boon, an imprint of HarperCollins*Publishers*
1 London Bridge Street, London, SE1 9GF

Large Print edition 2018

© 2018 Nina Milne

ISBN: 978-0-263-07416-1

MIX
Paper from
responsible sources
FSC™ C007454

This book is produced from independently certified
FSC™ paper to ensure responsible forest management.
For more information visit www.harpercollins.co.uk/green.

Printed and bound in Great Britain
by CPI Group (UK) Ltd, Croydon, CR0 4YY

To one of my very best friends,
who has proved the healing power of love.

CHAPTER ONE

MARCUS ALRIKSON LEANED back in the ergonomic comfort of the luxurious leather chair—his one extravagance in an office he spent way too much of his time in. But needs must when the devil drove. Even when the devil was his own personal demon—the one that ensured he never lost sight of the need to succeed.

Right now his focus was on ensuring that the royal wedding was a success. It could be argued that as Chief Advisor to the Prince of Lycander his remit didn't include wedding planning—and in truth the bride's dress and the groom's choice of tie didn't interest him in the slightest. The security of the royal nuptials, however, was very much his responsibility—after all alongside his role of Chief Advisor he also headed up Alrikson Security, a byword in security provision services across Europe.

There was also the fact that he had a great deal

of respect for Prince Frederick—the Prince was a good man, a ruler with a vision for the future of Lycander. A vision shared by Marcus.

He focused on the screen and studied his plan. His formidable brain assessed the risks, considered the most acute of angles, searched for the tiniest of chinks in the armour of defence and protocol that surrounded the upcoming wedding extravaganza.

In mere weeks Prince Frederick of Lycander would marry Sunita Bashwani-Greenberg, an ex-supermodel and mother of his two-year-old son Amil.

The union was a love-match that the people of Lycander had mixed feelings about. Frederick's ascent to the throne had been shrouded in tragedy and scandal, and it had taken him two years of fair and just rule even to begin the process of bringing the Lycandrian people round. And the throne still wobbled—Frederick had many enemies who would happily overthrow him and end Lycander's monarchy, enemies who would sabotage the wedding.

Not on Marcus's watch. It was crucial that this wedding went without a hitch.

B

WA

This book is to be returned on or before
the last date stamped below.

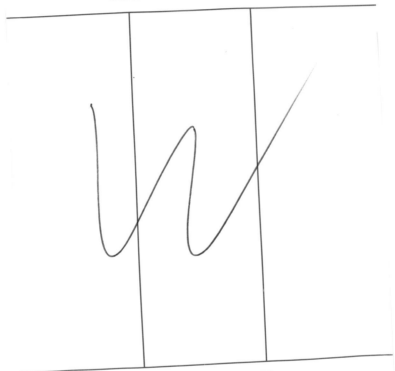

LEARNING FOR LIFE
LONDON BOROUGH OF SUTTON LIBRARIES

MAROONED
WITH THE
MILLIONAIRE

His frown intensified as he glared at the screen, looking up only when he heard a knock on the door.

'Come in.'

A rare smile touched his lips as his sister entered the room. 'Elvira.'

'Hey, big bro.'

'What can I do for you?'

As always he felt a profound relief when he saw his little sister, and a sense of gratitude that her life had worked out—that she seemed to have adjusted after her shaky start. Now twenty-two, she was content and successful and in her final year of studying law at university.

Speaking of which... His smile vanished. 'Shouldn't you be at lectures?'

'Relax. I'm free of lectures this morning. My tutor's ill, so I thought I'd drop in.'

He should have known Elvira wouldn't skip a lecture; for all his big-brother crackdown he knew that his sister took her studies seriously, and truly appreciated the opportunities life had granted her.

No, not life. Those opportunities had come courtesy of death—the death of their criminal, alcoholic, violent parents in a fire. The same fire that a twelve-year-old Marcus had rescued his younger sister from, the identical inferno he had failed to rescue his parents from. Jonny and Alicia Brockley had perished.

Marcus and Elvira had been adopted, and their lives had dramatically altered course. For the better. The knowledge was a permanent biting ache of guilt.

Marcus shook his head—now was not the moment for a trip down the ravaged and torturous twists of memory lane.

'Anything in particular on your mind?' he asked as he gestured for Elvira to sit, and waited as she curled up in the comfy chair he'd sequestered from one of the many rooms of the Lycander Palace. His office was a mishmash taken from the mounds of furniture stockpiled by previous royal incumbents.

'April Fotherington turned up at uni today… for "a chat".'

Marcus drummed his fingers on the desk in an irritated tattoo. April Fotherington was a writer for a popular upmarket celebrity magazine, and she was in the process of writing a feel-good ar-

ticle on the Lycander wedding. With an emphasis on *feel-good*. That had been the deal Marcus
had made with the magazine's editor-in-chief. In
person. Emphatically.

So a question begged. 'Why would April need
to have a chat with you? You don't know Frederick or Sunita.'

'She wasn't asking about them. She was asking about Axel. About the night of his death and
his relationship with Frederick.'

Damn it to hell.

Axel. He had been Marcus's best friend, Frederick's older brother, tragically killed in a car
crash two years before. 'Do you think she knows
anything?'

Elvira shrugged. 'I don't think she *knows* anything. But I think she suspects something is a bit
off—which is a problem. April Fotherington is
good at what she does and she may well pursue
this angle.'

'Did you give anything away?'

Elvira narrowed her eyes. 'Of course I didn't.
Give me *some* credit, Marcus.'

'Sorry—and I'm sorry you were put in this position.'

Frustrated anger welled inside him—the type that in his early years would have had him punching a wall. Now he had learnt to convert it into cold, hard determination.

'I'll deal with it. April won't bother you again.'

'Whoa—hold on.' Elvira frowned. 'Don't go overboard—all she did was ask a few questions, and I may be completely wrong to think she suspects anything. She was perfectly nice about it as well.'

'I get that. But I—'

'You hate that your little sister is involved in this. But it's not your fault. *Or* hers.'

Yet somehow it felt that way to him.

'Thank you, Elvi.' Marcus rose to his feet.

Elvira's brow creased into deeper grooves. 'Where are you going?'

He grabbed his leather jacket from the back of the chair and shrugged into it.

'I'm going to give you a lift to wherever you want to go, and then I am going to do my job and close April Fotherington down.'

April glanced down at her notebook, then up and around at her hotel room. Situated on the outskirts of Lycander's town centre, it was pleasant enough, though not extravagant—well within her editor's budgetary requirements. The room's impersonal anonymity suited her, being reminiscent of her own small London flat.

Chewing the end of her pencil, she stared down at the words she had written.

Fact One: Two years ago Axel, heir to the throne of Lycander, died in a fatal car crash after attending an official state function.

Fact Two: At said function Axel claimed that his younger brother Frederick had originally been asked to attend, and Axel had demanded to take his place.

Fact Three: Prince Frederick, then known as the Playboy Prince, instead attended a celebrity-packed party aboard a yacht.

Fact Four: In the here and now I have interviewed a political activist called Brian Sewell, who claims that, 'Axel should never have been there. Frederick bailed out at the last moment to attend some jet-setting party and Axel stepped up—just like he always did. Frederick didn't give a sh— Pardon me. He didn't give a damn about Lycander; he only

*cared about himself and his hedonistic life-
style. He should have died in that car crash,
not Axel. Axel didn't want to attend that function—he had other plans.'*

April's gaze lingered on the words *died* and
car crash and black despair threatened, jabbing
at every nerve-end, twisting her brain with jag-
ged flashes of memory.

Her baby son's face, his milky smell, the down
of his hair as a newborn, the first gummy smile,
the first toddling step… And then nothing. There
would be no more firsts. No more anything.

Because Edward had died in a car crash.

Her fault—the knowledge throbbed and pulsed
her brain.

*Fact One: I was planning on leaving my
husband, Edwards's father—Dean Stanworth.*

*Fact Two: Dean discovered my plans and
arrived home in a drunken violent fury,
snatched Edward and drove off.*

*Fact Three: He crashed, and both he and
Edward perished.*

Breathe, focus. She used all the tricks of the
grief trade, so carefully learned, and tried to

numb the pain. One last exhale and she was able to regard her notebook again, read the facts about Axel with structured dispassion. Able to block away the grief that clamoured behind the barricades.

The question now was: what next? Speak with Prince Frederick about it? No. Too soon. She needed further verification—after all, there was every chance her source was unreliable... Brian Sewell was a known anti-monarchist. Yet the intuition born of three years of dedication to her job—countless interviews—told her this was the truth.

Damn it.

She liked Frederick, she liked Sunita, and her commission was to write a happy piece—a feel-good fairy tale article that indicated belief in a happy-ever-after. April might not have achieved a happy-ever-after of her own, once the glitter had blown away her own personal fairy tale had decayed into a dark story of misery-ever-after. But that didn't mean she begrudged happiness to others. However—and there always seemed to *be* a 'however'—she believed in the truth.

If *she* had faced up to the truth earlier, tragedy might have been averted.

Relief swathed her as the phone rang, distracting her from another visit to the past. It was imperative she kept herself on track. Picking up the receiver, she identified herself.

'Good morning, Ms Fotherington.' The hotel receptionist's professional bell-like tone was clear. 'Marcus Alrikson is here for your meeting.'

Marcus Alrikson? Meeting?

April's mind slalomed, raced, whirred as she considered the words. For a start she did not *have* a meeting scheduled with Lycander's millionaire Chief Advisor, because he had made it crystal-clear that he didn't see any need for one.

April hadn't taken it personally—Marcus Alrikson hadn't given a single press interview in the past two years. He was a man who wielded massive influence and acted behind the scenes. Of course she knew about him. A self-made millionaire by the age of twenty-five, thanks to his start-up company, Alrikson Security, and from a privileged background. He'd attended a prestigious school where he'd met Prince Axel of

Lycander, and after Axel's death he'd been appointed Chief Advisor to Prince Frederick.

She'd *seen* him before too, of course, but only from a distance or in a photo, or in the very briefest of video clips as he strode through packs of reporters. Enough for her to garner the sense of a man who radiated an aura of tightly self-contained power, and to register the fact that he had the looks and build to wow the public, if he so wished.

Yet that desire was quite clearly *not* on the man's wish list—his expression always neutral with a veer towards grim.

So what was he doing here?

Clearly her meeting with his sister Elvira had rattled his cage.

Excellent.

'I'll be right down.'

Grabbing her oversized bag, she spared one glance at her reflection as she headed to the door. Good thing she always dressed 'business casual', and her wardrobe choices were simple. Today she'd opted for slim-leg trousers, a tucked-in shirt and a blazer. Sensible flat shoes. There was no need to do anything to her dark auburn hair; her chosen style was short, sleek and easy to maintain.

So she was ready to face whatever Marcus might throw at her—and she had no doubt there would be something. Marcus Alrikson was anti-press, and if he was here that meant his feathers had been seriously ruffled.

The lift took her down to the marble lobby, and she crossed to the curved reception desk and nearly screeched to halt. The man standing there was...*gorgeous*.

Those glimpses of him, those images, couldn't have prepared her for the reality of Marcus Alrikson in the flesh. Or for her visceral reaction to him. Her tummy twisted and her hormones fizzed out of their deep hibernation mode with a suddenness that had her brain at panic stations. Shock slowed her steps further.

April didn't *do* attraction; her hormones hadn't so much as whispered in the past years. In fact forget hibernation—she'd been pretty sure her hormones were stone-cold dead. And that had been fine by her. The fuse of attraction could set off a chain reaction that ended in misery—that was a life lesson she'd learnt. So *this* fuse was being doused right now.

Marcus's eyebrows rose and he raised his hand in salute.

Get a grip and get moving!

As she headed towards him she reminded herself that she'd interviewed princes and billionaires, Hollywood A-listers and models. But, dammit, this man had a presence that had nothing to do with his undeniable wealth, status, or even his equally undeniable good-looks: dark unruly hair, a shade overlong, midnight-blue eyes, a firm jaw, and a strong nose that looked as if it might have broken at some point.

OK. So he was good-looking. But that wasn't the point. The point was the story—and she'd clearly provoked concern at the very least or he wouldn't be here. Yet he didn't look remotely worried, or angry, though there was a sense of taut energy in his stance—an energy she sensed was his perpetual state, a part of who he was.

'Mr Alrikson.'

There was a moment, a fleeting instant, when his expression registered the tiniest glimmer of surprise. Surprise and something else—his dark gaze had rested on her face, something had flickered and her treacherous body had responded, craving to move nearer to him.

Staunchly she kept her feet planted on the floor. 'This is unexpected.'

'Yes, it is.' He frowned, as if the words had escaped of their own volition. Then, 'Please, call me Marcus.'

She inclined her head, knowing that common courtesy indicated a need to shake hands. But she didn't want to. Stupid, she knew, but her body's reaction to him had caught her utterly off guard, wrong-footed her enough that it was a relief not to be in heels.

This was ridiculous. Her distrust of good-looking men was based on experience of the bitter kind. Handsome men had a different perspective on life—a belief that they were God's gift, and an easy arrogance that could lead to less than desirable character traits.

Never judge a book by its cover was a saying she believed in wholeheartedly.

'Marcus. I wasn't aware that we'd scheduled a meeting. In fact I am certain we didn't, because you made it very clear that you felt there was no need to meet me. Instead you very kindly had your office give me this scintillating quote: "I wish the couple every happiness".'

Easy does it, April.

She really did have to get a grasp of events. If she could pull off an interview with Marcus it would be a journalistic coup. So antagonising him was a rookie error she could ill afford. Blaming Marcus for throwing her into a loop-the-loop was foolish in the extreme.

'Yup. That about covers it.' Any initial response to her was clearly under control now, and his voice was an easy, deep drawl.

'So why are you here?'

'Because I thought you had been commissioned to write a feel-good article on the Lycander wedding—with an exclusive focus on the happy couple.'

'Yes. That's correct.'

'So why did you feel the need to accost my sister?'

'"Accost" is a strong word. I simply spoke with her.'

'Accost is an entirely *accurate* word. You accosted her at her university campus without any attempt to schedule a meeting.'

'I thought she might be helpful in shedding light on an…an angle I have come across.'

'I find that hard to believe. Elvira is barely acquainted with either the Prince *or* Sunita.'

'As I said, it's a different angle.'

'So I gather—and I look forward to hearing exactly what that angle is.'

April's mind weighed and discarded options. Her intuition that Elvira had been hiding something seemed vindicated now that here in front of her was a main player. But perhaps the most sensible option would be to decline to cross swords with a man who was undoubtedly a master fencer. Instead she should take this as tacit confirmation that there was some truth to her suspicions and pursue her investigation.

'I'm afraid I'm not ready to share yet.'

'I'm afraid that isn't acceptable.'

Now it was her turn to raise her eyebrows. 'Is that a threat?'

'Of course not. It's an observation. I have a deal with your magazine—if you are in the process of reneging on that deal then I have the right to know. Both the Prince and Sunita have more than co-operated with you thus far, as have various palace officials. That co-operation will cease.'

A part of her knew she should be jubilant—he *must* be rattled. Yet he didn't look it—instead he looked utterly at ease…a man who believed he was in control of the situation.

'Sounds like a threat to me.'

'Not at all. Consider it a negotiation. Why don't I buy you a coffee and we can discuss terms?'

A sudden jolt of anticipation shot a frisson of awareness through her. On some stupid level she *wanted* this skirmish, and she knew the reasons why were more complex than her pursuit of an angle to a story. She had the horrible feeling it had something to do with the insidious tug of awareness her brain was desperately trying to shut down.

'Let's go,' she said.

CHAPTER TWO

MARCUS FORCED HIS expression to remain neutral. No way did he want to project any of the disquiet that had surfaced inside him. April had a reputation as being a writer with integrity; her articles never gossiped—or if they did the gossip was fact not rumour or speculation. Which was exactly why anyone with a secret to hide hoped to slip under her radar.

Unfortunately the Prince of Lycander *did* have a secret, and it looked as though April Fotherington's radar was abuzz. The angle she was in hot pursuit of was exactly the slope he *didn't* want her to climb. Because at the summit lay political disaster.

That was what he needed to focus on…shame his body had other ideas. One look at April and *va-va-voom*—he'd been worried his eyeballs would pop out on cartoon springs. Her beauty was undeniable, and yet he couldn't quite identify what it was about her that had caused such an intense tug of desire. Especially when she represented a danger to everything he had worked for over the past few years.

Perhaps it was best not to analyse the situation, or he might give in to the desire to study her at greater length, absorb her natural grace as she walked slightly ahead of him, check out the length of her legs, the slender span of her waist, the dark auburn of her hair that tapered onto the delicate nape of her neck...

Whoa. What was wrong with him? Right now April classed as the enemy, and his focus needed to be on shutting down this story—not ogling the opposition.

And so he continued through the lobby, eyes focused firmly above her head as they entered the hotel restaurant now nigh on empty in the post-breakfast pre-lunch lull. Scanning the room, he picked the optimum table—one that granted privacy and the opportunity to check the room for potential eavesdroppers.

He strode across the plush carpeted floor to a corner table, flanked by walls and potted greenery. A waiter materialised, pulled out chairs and proffered a menu, which Marcus waved away.

'I'll have a double espresso.'

'Latte for me, please,' April supplied.

He allowed himself to study her for a moment, telling himself it was a simple assessment to enable him to read her better. And if it unsettled her a little—well, all the better.

Dark auburn hair framed a heart-shaped face. Vivid green eyes of a colour he had never seen before—darker and softer than emerald—brought to mind forests and elven folklore. Her face held an allure that she seemed genuinely unaware of—there was no attempt at being coy, nor any overt flirtatiousness in her body language. And yet he could sense a simmer of awareness—the type of awareness that made his gaze linger a little too long on her generous lips, on the graceful tilt of her neck...

Stop. Get with the plan.

The point was to unsettle April, not himself. This situation was dangerous, and he needed to keep focused on what was important. April Fotherington's lips definitively did *not* come under that category.

'So…' he said.

'So?' she returned.

'Why don't you tell me what your angle is?'

Tipping her head slightly to one side, she contemplated him. No doubt wondering how little she could disclose and get away with.

Seeing the waiter approach, he raised a hand. 'Hang on. Our coffee's here.'

They both waited in silence as their drinks were carefully deposited in front of them, and then for a few more beats until the waiter was out of earshot.

'Go ahead,' he said.

She blew out an exaggerated puff of air. 'Telling you is a non-starter. Once I tell you, you'll try and kill the story.'

'Yes. We both know that. But if you *don't* tell me you'll lose all access to the Prince and his bride and we'll call in a different magazine.'

A frown creased her forehead. 'Isn't this overkill? All I've done is have a chat to your sister.'

'Not true, April, and we both know it. You also met with Brian Sewell.'

The anger he'd felt at that discovery resurfaced,

and he forced his body to remain relaxed, his voice almost casual.

Her whole body stilled, but other than that she gave no indication of guilt. 'Yes, I did.'

'Did you approach him?'

'No. He approached me. I understand he is a great proponent of democracy and I wanted a different perspective to put into the article. I won't apologise for that.'

'I'm not asking for an apology. I'm asking you not to pursue whatever line he has cast.'

Green eyes met his with cool aplomb. 'I can't do that. If there is a story there I need to follow it.'

'Even if it isn't the story you have been commissioned to write?'

'Maybe it's a better story.'

'And that's all you care about, isn't it? The story? Circulation? Your reputation? And never mind the collateral damage.'

'No!' Her eyes flashed sparks at him as she pushed her cup away and leant across the table. 'I care about the truth. And if this story is true then clearly all *you* care about is covering up the truth.'

'I will tell you exactly what I care about. I care about Lycander. I care about my country and its people.'

'Then surely you believe that "your" people deserve the truth? That is all I want to discover. The truth.'

The fervour with which she spoke was quiet but absolute, and for a second it caused him to pause.

'Then perhaps you should choose your sources more carefully.'

'Meaning…?'

'Meaning Brian Sewell is not exactly a credible source. Plus, as I heard it, he was pretty plastered at your lunch yesterday—I'm not sure his drunken ramblings will stand up to scrutiny.'

Her green eyes narrowed and her entire body vibrated with outrage. 'Are you *spying* on me?'

'No. But I *am* keeping tabs on Brian Sewell. He is a dissident of the worst type.'

'There is no crime in being a dissident.'

'No, but there *is* a crime in organising and encouraging violent rallies—mobs made up of people who simply want an excuse to legitimise violence and mayhem.'

'Then why haven't you arrested him?'

Because the man was more slippery than a jellied eel. He played the part of a concerned citizen who simply wished to advocate a voice for democracy to perfection, but in reality he was no more than the leader of a criminal gang of nutters.

'Nothing would give me greater pleasure, believe me, and as soon as I have a watertight case against him Sewell *will* be behind bars.'

'Well, I believe a man is innocent until proved guilty, and right now Brian Sewell looks perfectly credible to me.'

'Brian Sewell is dangerous and manipulative.'

She snorted—there was no other word for it.

'Please give me *some* credit. I am not an idiot and I have no intention of being manipulated. If his claims don't stack up I won't publish them—or even refer to them in any form.'

'By then it may be too late—Sewell has spun you a web of dirt, and dirt sticks. To investigate you will have to ask questions, and then the story will gain momentum—the type of momentum that people like Sewell will harness. Then it won't matter whether it is true or not—the ramifications for Frederick will be huge, as well as casting a blight over his wedding.'

She shook her head. 'This still doesn't make sense. I get that you may be worried—but *this* worried? You must have to deal with stuff like this all the time. There must be plenty of people opposed to the monarchy, and I am quite sure you are more than capable of dealing with them and their stories. You've got your tightie-whities in a knot over this one because you think I may have something explosive—something *true*.'

There was a pause—then horror etched her face, along with a tinge of disbelief, and despite the seriousness of the conversation a smile tipped his lips.

'Lucky for me, I don't wear tightie-whities.'

The flush deepened and he knew with crystal clarity that she was wondering exactly what he *did* wear... And suddenly he couldn't help but wonder the same about her. Her gaze meshed with his and awareness swirled the air.

Then she shook her head. 'I don't think your choice of underwear is salient right now. Or ever will be,' she added hurriedly.

She was so very right. Irritation sloughed over his skin. What the *hell* was he doing?

'The bottom line is that if Brian Sewell is telling the truth then I have a duty to disclose that truth.' She looked at him. 'But I'll tell you what I can offer.' She leant forward. 'Why don't you put your money where your mouth is? I'll interview *you*. You can comment on Brian Sewell's claims. If they aren't true then tell me flat-out that he's lying.' Her eyes were intent now. 'I am not after dirt. I don't want to blacken anyone's name or cause unnecessary harm or distress with salacious rumour. That's not what I do. I want the truth. So let me question *you* on the record about Brian Sewell's comments.'

For an insane moment he was tempted—to explain the truth and trust April to see that decisions that had been made on the back of guilt, misery and tragedy had been made for the greater good. Decisions had been made to cover up the truth not because anyone had done anything wrong, but because the truth might have resulted in the overthrow of the monarchy.

Prince Frederick *should* have been at that state function, and he *had* bailed out at the last minute because he'd wanted to attend a party to celebrate pulling off an amazing business coup. Axel had agreed to attend in his place and had decided to pretend that *he* had instigated the swap in order to show Frederick in a more favourable light.

Then had come the tragedy—on leaving the dinner Axel had been involved in a fatal car crash. If the people of Lycander had discovered that it should have been Frederick in that car they might have lynched him, and the monarchy might well have been overthrown. So there *had* been a cover-up. He had no idea how Sewell had got hold of the information, but he had. Maybe he had simply hazarded a lucky guess...but there it was—the less than shining truth.

He squashed the crazy, inexplicable temptation to share it. Surely he was too experienced to be hoodwinked by a pair of intense green eyes? How could he trust her? He barely knew her. Yes, perhaps she would reveal the truth in a sympathetic way, but it was too big a risk to take. Marcus would not throw everything and everyone he held dear to wolves and vermin like Sewell.

Prince Frederick of Lycander cared about his land and his people, and he was slowly but surely bringing Lycander back to a place of prosperity and fairness for all. The truth was not an option. Equally, though, there was no way he would lie—he'd be a fool thrice over to lie to a writer of April's calibre.

So, neither the truth nor a lie…

'No can do,' he said easily. 'I don't do interviews—under *any* circumstances. I won't make an exception to that rule, but I *will* show you why I think you should drop this story.'

Her brow creased in puzzlement. 'Show me?'

He rose to his feet, hitched his wallet from his jacket pocket and put some money on the table. 'Come with me. I'm going to take you on a tour.'

Her brow creased. 'A tour?'

'Yup.'

Her eyes narrowed in clear suspicion. 'Why? I don't get it. You're a busy man. Wouldn't it be easier to just answer some questions?'

'No. The minute I go on record this story gains publicity and credibility. You know it. I know it. So I'd rather do this differently.'

'What happened to the threats?'

'I'd prefer to try the civilised way first.' Because, whatever she was, she wasn't a run-of-the-mill writer or a gossip columnist. 'What do you say?'

Head tilted to one side, she considered, then nodded. 'OK. I'm intrigued. Let's go.'

A couple of phone calls later they exited the hotel lobby. What else could she have said? April mused as she pushed through the revolving door. No writer would have turned down the opportunity of a surprise tour from Marcus Alrikson. Problem was, she had a sneaking suspicion that no *woman* would turn it down either, and she had misgivings as to whether it was the writer or the woman in her that had acquiesced.

The writer, of course. It couldn't be any other way. The very *idea* of being attracted to Marcus Alrikson—to any man—made her shiver in repudiation. Never again. That side of her life had been laid waste and would remain desolate through her own choice. If her hormones were foolish enough to try for resurrection she would mow them down without hesitation.

'Where are we going?' she enquired as they walked along increasingly tourist-thronged pavements towards the city centre.

Marcus gestured around. 'What do you see?'

'A shopping mecca for those who love fashion.'

Designer names abounded—clothes most people could only dream of called out to those with money to burn or credit cards to burden.

His dark blue eyes scanned her outfit, swept her body from top to toe, and to her own irritation she blushed. Then his gaze returned to hers and a funny little thrill shot through her veins at the expression in his eyes—a smoulder that she knew she hadn't imagined.

'It sounds like you aren't one of their number.'

Sounds or *looks*? For an instant a stupid part of her bridled at his judgement, even though it was spot-on.

'No. I'm not.'

Once she had been intent on always looking good, because Dean had insisted on it. He'd wanted his wife to be 'a credit' to him—wanted every man in the room to envy him.

Standing there in the heat of the Lycandrian sun April froze…could almost hear Dean's rich Southern drawl. At the time she had taken his words as a sign of his pride in her, too smitten to see the truth—that to Dean she'd been a trophy, a prize and nothing more. So she'd made sure her clothes were the latest fashion, the most expensive and exclusive brands, had spent hours in the hairdressers, at the gym, putting on make-up. But now...

'I try to be professional, but that's as far as it goes. As part of my job I do keep up with the latest trends. Readers like details on what people are wearing.' She waved a hand around. 'Whilst I'm not a shopper, I appreciate the appeal to the rich.'

'And a big part of Lycander's economy relies on attracting the rich and the glamorous to our shores. We *want* designer names—we *want* the tourists and the parties. But we can't *only* cater for the celebrity crowd. We need to look after our own people. So now I want to show you a different side of Lycander.'

A sleek black chauffeured car pulled up to the kerb and April climbed in first, forcing herself not to scrunch up as close to the window as possible to lessen their proximity. *Daft*. This had to stop—right now she needed to concentrate, to determine whether or not this was some complicated political manoeuvre to persuade her to abandon her pursuit of the truth.

The truth—that was what was important. Ever since the tragedy in which she'd lost Edward, after she'd clawed her way out of the pit of despair, she'd vowed never to sidestep the truth.

She watched the Lycander landscape flash by, saw the busy, prosperous streets recede and slowly morph into roads on a sliding scale of prosperity that eventually spiralled downwards, until a sense of squalor gradually pervaded. Buildings became less well maintained, shops became smaller and dingier, walls were scratched with the bright slash of graffiti. And as the miles were swallowed up soon the designer-laden city centre seemed like a bubble, an impossible dream.

Aware of his watchful gaze, she turned her head and saw the intensity of his expression. His face was suddenly harder, shadowed with grimness, his blue eyes dark with purpose.

'When you think of Lycander, what images come to mind?' he asked. 'Other than that of a designer paradise, with yachts and jet-setters.'

'Exports. Olives, wine and lemons. Beaches. Casinos. Wealth.'

'Yes. All that exists. And under Prince Alphonse the casinos and rich celebrity hordes thrived. But he took the money they generated and instead of spending it on the country spent it on himself. He taxed the olives, the lemons, the vineyards, and he squandered the money on his lavish lifestyle. He squandered his people's future.'

'But…but surely someone could have stopped him?'

'No. In Lycander, the ruler's word is law.'

'Then Brian Sewell has a point. The monarchy sucks.'

'It depends on the ruler. Obviously Lycander's fortunes are linked to the ruler's morality and capabilities. History shows that overall the good times have outweighed the bad—most rulers have truly cared and ruled with justice.'

'But Alphonse didn't?'

'No. But Axel would have, and Frederick does. Or at least he is trying to.' He shrugged. 'Perhaps one day democracy *will* be the right way forward—perhaps Frederick himself will decide to make those changes. But now is not the time. Lycander is not ready.'

'What gives *you* the right to decide that?'

'Nothing. It is not my decision—it is my *belief.*
And I will fight for that belief.'

'Then maybe you should let Brian Sewell fight
for his.'

'Through inciting violence and riots? Through
a campaign of rumour and mire?'

'OK. Not Brian Sewell. But those who believe
that a ruler should be elected...shouldn't be given
such immense power simply through birth and
blood.'

'Lycander has had a monarchy for centuries,
and on the whole it has worked. Right now it *is*
working. But there is an enormous amount of
work to do, and Frederick is the man to do it.'

'Frederick—or you?' The words came unbidden, ignited by the sheer determination in his
voice.

'Frederick is the Prince and he has a vision that
I share. It is my honour to be of help to him.'

'And if you and he disagree on policy? What
happens then?'

Marcus shook his head. 'This isn't an interview, April.'

'I know that. This is off the record.'

Marcus snorted. 'But if you quote that "a leading figure in Frederick's council" privately said blah-blah-blah, I'm sure people will join the dots.'

'I won't quote anything you don't want to be quoted.'

'That's what you say now, but if our relationship goes downhill you may change your mind. For the record, I don't want to be quoted. Period. What I *do* want is for you to drop the story.'

'You still haven't shown me why.'

'*This* is why.'

He gestured out of the window and April turned her head.

Now they were in a different place all together. The streets were grubby, poverty was pervasive. Shops were shuttered, broken windows and rusted corrugated iron denoted a desolation that was a world away from lemons, olives and wine.

'This is the result of Alphonse's rule, and this is what Frederick wants to turn around. But to do that we need time—time that can't be taken by a democratic, political fund-sucking fight.'

He leant forward and murmured to the driver, and two minutes later the car pulled to a stop.

'I want to show you what we're trying to do.'

CHAPTER THREE

MARCUS ALIGHTED FROM the car and April scooted across the seat after him, emerged and looked around.

This area was different again—not like the plush wealth of the city, nor the high glitz of Lycander's high life, but it had an air of hope, shown by the green of a park, the few small cafés and shops that weren't boarded up. One large building had a fresh coat of paint and boxes of flowers on the windowsills. The sound of music came from inside and the front doors were wide open. Groups of youths chatted outside, clustered in the sunshine.

'This is a newly founded community centre. We opened it seven months ago, with funds from Lycander's coffers and overseas help from the Caversham Foundation.'

April nodded. 'Set up and run by Ethan and Ruby Caversham.'

'I read your interview with them.'

'They are incredible people.'

They truly were—April had warmed to the couple and their genuine belief in the foundation they ran for troubled teenagers.

'Yes, and they helped us with money and, equally importantly, with advice.' Marcus shrugged. 'It takes more than money to get something like this to work. Teenagers have to *want* to come here, and they need to come here not to fight and continue gang warfare but because they want to help implement change.'

Before she could respond a group of five teenagers headed towards them, with more than a hint of swagger, and April stepped a little closer to Marcus. Big mistake. Strength emanated from him, and the sheer solidity of him, the scent of leather and a woodsy overtone, almost made her mewl.

Without subtlety she leapt sideways—she'd take her chances with the youths, who she could now see didn't actually seem any threat. In fact she'd swear their studied nonchalance disguised pleasure.

'Hey, Marcus.'

'Blake.' Marcus stepped forward and the two exchanged some sort of complicated handshake.

'You here to train?'

'Not today.' Marcus shook his head. 'I'm here to show April around—she's a writer. April, this is Blake and Gemma, Jacob, Aurelie and Isaac.'

'Why'd you bring *her* here?' The suspicion in Gemma's voice would have curdled milk. 'She's a gossip columnist. She won't be interested in the likes of us.'

'I'm a writer,' April interjected. 'I'm interested in all aspects of Lycander.'

'Not just this ridiculous, showy waste of money royal wedding?' Blake said. 'And the so-called perfection of the Prince and his bride? My family can't afford food whilst *they* squander millions on fireworks.'

Gemma shook her head emphatically, her bright blonde hair swishing in disagreement. 'You need to look at the bigger picture, Blake. Sure, they're spending a whole heap of money—but solely on Lycandrian goods, which will bring in loads of revenue to Lycander. Revenue that Frederick will put back into the system to benefit the people, so that your family and mine won't have to rely on food banks.'

'Charity.' There was no disguise for the bitterness in Blake's voice as he kicked at the kerbside. 'People say that we're layabouts and criminals, but what are we *supposed* to do?'

Isaac weighed in. 'Accept the benefits on offer. Frederick has set up free courses. My dad has enrolled on a mechanics programme. Once he qualifies, maybe he'll be given a chance at a better life.'

'That's one man out of thousands.'

'No one said change can happen overnight. It's a start.'

The debate continued and April glanced at Marcus, who had taken no part in the discussion. He simply leant against a wall and watched with interest, respect and definite pride. He caught her gaze and for a long moment held it, his dark blue eyes intent. She gave a near shiver—not of fear, but of sheer attraction.

Pushing off the wall, he asked, 'So what do you all think of having a democracy?'

Gemma shrugged. 'If you'd asked me two years ago when Axel died I'd have said yes.'

At the mention of Axel, April sensed a small movement next to her and turned her head, caught the flash of pain fleeting across Marcus's dark blue eyes, the shadow of grief and loss. Not obvious, but evident to her. Hell, she could smell grief a mile off—sniff it out with the bitter sense of personal experience.

Without thought she moved a little closer to him, in an instinctive desire to offer sympathy as they listened to Gemma.

'Because I believed Frederick would be a repeat of Alphonse—a playboy rather than a tyrant, a ruler who wouldn't care about Lycander. But he promised that he would follow Axel's policies, and so far he has. So right now I'm happy to give him a chance. But only if he is the real deal—if it turns out this is all a con, a ploy, a lie, then I'll be on the streets in protest.'

'So,' April asked, 'who here and now would vote for a democracy?'

By now more people had gathered, and there was a hum as the question circulated.

'Those for?'

Hands were raised, but nowhere near as many as April would have expected.

'Those against?' Now there was a sea of hands, including Blake's.

The discussion continued, and it was clear the group had forgotten that April was even there.

She turned to Marcus. 'Interesting.'

'Sure is. Because if you had seen a lot of these teens a few months ago they wouldn't have cared. That's part of the problem—sheer apathy or a mindless belief of the kind Brian Sewell encourages. He takes people's rightful dissatisfaction with the system and turns it into hatred and violence.'

'Whereas here you encourage people to think about it. And that is interesting too.'

'In what way?'

'It's *you*, isn't it? This is *your* project, your input. I saw how those kids looked at you—they care about your opinion and I saw how proud you are of them.'

There was a pause and she couldn't help it—she grinned.

'You're blushing.'

'I am not blushing.'

'Yes, you are.' Without thought she reached up. 'Right there.'

Lord knew she meant to point at his cheek, but somehow along the line the wires got crossed between her brain and her fingers and instead she brushed her hand down the angle of his cheekbone, along the firm line of his jaw tinged with early-afternoon shadow.

Her breath caught in her throat and for too long—*way* too long—her hand remained against his skin. Until finally her brain caught up with events and panic descended, sending the order to snatch her fingers away.

Unfortunately the panic also took a stranglehold on her vocal cords and no words, no excuses, no witty quip came to her lips.

'Now I think it's *you* who may be blushing.'

His deep voice caressed her skin and then he lifted a hand and oh-so-gently trailed a finger down her own cheek. Her tummy clenched at the hot flash of desire that shot through her.

'Right there.'

It was a good thing he didn't know that right now he'd be hard put to find a part of her body that *wasn't* flushed with heat. An image of his finger continuing its trail streamed through her brain and she closed her eyes and summoned up the power of common sense.

Hadn't she learnt her lesson? Learnt how attraction could deceive and twist and lead her astray? *Enough.* This man had a goal—to keep her from her story—and maybe his intent now was to distract her from her purpose.

Moving backwards, she summoned a rictus smile. But as she forced herself to look at him she saw his expression was as full of horror as her own, and she knew that whatever had just happened Marcus's surprise equalled her own.

That hadn't been a strategic move by Lycander's Chief Advisor—in fact he looked as flummoxed as she felt. He, however, was recovering considerably quicker.

'Right. We seem to have got distracted by a blushing contest. I declare it a draw. Now, why don't I show you around the inside of the centre?'

He nodded towards the group of teens, who were still deep in conversation.

'For the record, these kids are Lycander's future, and I want them to have a future that doesn't include seeing the inside of a prison. They deserve a lot more than that.'

His words pulled her into reality, brought her focus back. She nodded, deciding that the best way to go was to expel the whole memory of the past few minutes and erase it from her timeline. Hard, though, when her skin still tingled. She tried to concentrate solely on her surroundings, creating a memory of the image because she knew that this was a place she would like to write about.

April could see the thought that had been put into the interior of the centre, the efforts to make it look less institutional and more 'homelike'. No doubt a lot of the youths here didn't have the best home life, and so would appreciate the comfy sofas and recliner chairs and bean bags, the television and the well-stocked bookshelves, the up-to-date magazines stacked on tables.

There was a gym, a room with a pool table, a ping-pong table and then, after going down a corridor, they entered a room that contained a boxing ring.

'Boxing?' April tried to keep the disapproval from her voice.

'Yes. Training is a great way to let off steam. There's a whole lot of illegal boxing that goes on in the streets—the kind that can actually kill. I want this to be somewhere kids can come and pursue boxing safely.'

'But it's dangerous and violent and…'

'It's a sport. One that requires discipline and dedication. Danger and violence is on the streets.'

'So, do *you* box?'

'Yes.'

Heaven help her—because April certainly couldn't help herself. An image of him stripped down, training with a punch bag, his muscles a testimony to discipline and dedication, shot across her mind.

'Why?' she managed, her reporter's instincts coming to her rescue. 'What's the appeal?'

'I started in my teens.'

His tone was less than forthcoming, and it wasn't really an answer.

'In fact it was boxing that started this place off. I set up a fight, offered to take anyone on in a one-on-one. I thought it would give them an incentive to come here.'

April stared at him. 'And the best incentive you could come up with was to offer yourself up as a target?' Horror touched her. 'Couldn't you have brought someone else in?'

'I could've—but it wouldn't have been as effective. I wanted to get their attention, show them that I'm more than some flash millionaire politician trying to rule over them. So, yes, I put myself on the line.'

He smiled suddenly and April blinked—the smile transformed his face, lit his dark blue eyes with a glint of amusement, and her toes twitched in her sensible flat navy shoes.

'Don't look so aghast. I'm actually pretty good.'

'Yes, but you were up against fighters who might bend the rules. You could have been seriously hurt.'

She knew they were talking about teenagers, here, but she was pretty sure that a lot of the youths on the streets might be short on years but would be long on experience.

'It was worth the risk. It got people here. A huge crowd, in fact, who stayed when it was over and listened to what I had to say about what was going to be on offer here. You heard Blake—these people are poor, but they have their pride. Most of them don't want hand-outs. They wouldn't have come here otherwise.'

'What happened?'

'I won. It was bloody, but the fights were fair. All but one, where the kid pulled a knife and got turfed out—not by me, but by the crowd. Three fights, and at the end they were willing to listen. The next day some of them came back, the day after a few more, and slowly… I think it's working.'

His voice, the sheer force of his belief and zeal, held her mesmerised. As she looked around the ring she could picture the scene, hear the drip of blood on the canvas, the silence and the cheers of the crowds, the aura of grit and the focus of the fighters. Most of all she could see Marcus—a man willing quite literally to fight for his beliefs, to endure pain in order to win victory for others.

The idea took her breath away, made her feel a little light-headed even as she wondered why. What drove him to this? Grief over his best friend? A need to propel Axel's vision into reality? Perhaps, but she thought there must be more to it. Whatever it was, she was damn sure he wouldn't tell *her*.

'I think it's working too,' she agreed. 'Those kids are all thinking, and they all care one way or another. And they are all here.'

She followed him down another long corridor towards the unmistakable scent of food and the sizzle of onions and chips.

'I'll show you the canteen and then we'll be on our way,' Marcus said.

They entered a spacious room, complete with wooden tables and benches, one of which was being polished by a young girl April reckoned couldn't be much older than seventeen.

'Hey, Mia.'

Marcus's voice was gentle, and the girl looked up and gave him a shy smile.

'Hi.' She straightened up.

'Getting ready for the hordes to arrive for lunch?'

She nodded.

April walked forward with Marcus and smiled.

'Mia, this is April. She's a writer. April, this is Mia. And this…'

Mia had bent over, and too late April spotted the pram next to the bench. Mia scooped an infant out.

'This is Charlie,' Mia said softly, her face alight with pride.

April froze, caught wrong-footed, and desperately tried to remember all the defence mechanisms she'd learnt—how to shield herself when it was impossible to avoid a baby.

Marcus stepped forward and the baby gave an impossibly sweet gummy grin of excitement.

'Charlie loves Marcus,' Mia said as Charlie tumbled forward, clearly desperate for Marcus to take him.

Even through the descent of grief April registered that Marcus seemed very comfortable with the baby, holding him with the impression of ease and making quacking noises that elicited a stream of giggles from Charlie.

The sound twisted April's heart. She could feel the room begin to spin and desperately tried to distance herself, to shut down her emotions before they became too hard to hold. It would usually be fine, but this had taken her by surprise—and, worse, Charlie had a real look of Edward about him. The same colour hair, tufted up into little spikes, the same gurgle in his laugh, the same chubby legs…

If she held very still she could almost allow herself to imagine for one wonderful moment that it *was* Edward.

Nearly as soon as it had come the illusion vanished, leaving behind tears of sadness. Somehow she held it together. 'He is gorgeous.' The tremble in her voice would hopefully pass without comment—and yet she was aware that Marcus's forehead had creased into a watchful expression.

'Thank you,' Mia said as she took Charlie back from Marcus. 'I need to go and check on the menu. It was nice to meet you. Wave to Marcus, Charlie.'

Relief flooded April as Mia walked away. Time to pull herself together. A few years ago that would have been impossible. But now she could do it—she *would* do it.

Her family had helped her put herself back together in the dark aftermath of Edward's death, and she would not let them or herself down by returning to that black pit of despair. Instead she would focus on her life, her job, her future. The existence she had mapped out for herself, in which she had found a level of peace.

'Are you OK?'

Marcus's voice was gruff with a concern that both warmed her and made more tears threaten.

'I'm fine.'

His frown deepened. 'Are you sure? You looked as though you'd been sucker-punched straight in the chest and left down for the count.'

An apt description—not that she would admit it.

'I'm not in the boxing ring, Marcus, and last I looked there wasn't anyone throwing their fists around. It must have been a trick of the light. I'm completely fine.' She glanced at her watch. 'Now, I'm afraid I need to get back. I can get a cab. Thank you for the tour—I really appreciate it. It's given me a lot to think about.'

'Whoa. Hang on.'

Dark blue eyes studied her face and she forced herself to hold his gaze. The grief was under control now, but harder to leash was her awareness of him, of the fact that his gaze seemed to heat her skin.

'I'm glad you're OK, and I'm glad you enjoyed the tour. Can I take it that you'll drop the story?'

Her eyes narrowed. 'No, you can't. I said you've

given me a lot to think about—that implies I need to go away and *think*.'

For a second she thought he'd argue; instead he nodded, though she could see reluctance etched on his face.

'Fair enough. Then let's meet tomorrow. Would lunchtime suit you? Say twelve-thirty?'

There it was again—that silly, stupid thrill of anticipation at the thought of seeing Marcus again. Madness. But no matter. After tomorrow there would be no need to see him again. Whatever decision she came to.

'That's fine.'

CHAPTER FOUR

MARCUS REREAD THE paragraph outlining fiscal policy for the third time, uttered a curse, and shoved the bound folder across his desk, oblivious to the dappled rays of golden Lycandrian morning sunshine or the sweet smell of mimosa that wafted in from outside.

If only he was as immune to images of April Fotherington. Yet her image intruded with persistence, flitting across his brain and pushing out the facts in the report.

Foolish! She wasn't even his type. Insofar as he even *had* a type. Sure, she was attractive, but he had met plenty of attractive women in his time and none had had the ability to distract him from work. He had a work ethic that had driven him from the moment of his adoption—an iron determination to make something of his life. To atone for the night of the fire, and to make a difference in the world.

He'd figured out that to do that he needed money, so he'd built up his business and attained millionaire status. Now he was determined to help Frederick bring about change to Lycander—and he would *not* let an attraction stand in the way of that.

Perhaps it wasn't an attraction…

Hah, Marcus—really?

Maybe, his brain persisted, his subconscious was trying to warn him that this woman was a threat, an adversary he needed to defeat rather than a woman he wanted to…

Wanted to what? Have a relationship with? He didn't *do* relationships. Sleep with? Not happening. April was not his sort of woman…not an anonymous, discreet ship passing in the night, the type of woman who would never expect more than the very little he could offer: a brief interlude, physical release, and then moving on without regret.

There was a vulnerability about April, and despite her denial the previous day he sensed that she had demons that could vie with his own. And that meant she was so far off-limits she might as well be in a different stratosphere.

Pulling the report back towards him, he tackled paragraph three again, glaring the words into submission. Sheer will-power propelled him through the report, two meetings and a visit to the head office of Alrikson Security. But images of April filtered the net of his determination for the duration, and en route to pick her up he felt a strange, fizzy thread of anticipation run through his gut, followed by a bubbling doubt.

Why had he asked her to lunch? Yes, he needed to see her, but he could have done that in his office. Why make it a lunch date? Date? No. *Meeting*—that was the word.

Oh, God. It was time to get a grip. April represented a threat to Lycander he needed to eliminate. End of. He would do whatever it took to ensure his country was given the chance to return to prosperity. It was inconceivable that something as petty as physical attraction should get in the way of that.

Yet as the car pulled up outside the hotel with its bright awning and gilded doors, and he spotted April outside, clad in dark tailored trousers and a dove-grey short-sleeved blouse, his body tensed. His nerves went on alert in recognition of the kind of primal magnetic pull no amount of will-power could eradicate—a tug as far from petty as it was possible to be.

Fine. If he couldn't eliminate it he would ignore it, conceal it, fight it...

A frown etching his forehead, he climbed out of the car and moved round to open the door for her. 'Hi,' he managed.

'Hi.'

For a moment, he would have sworn he'd glimpsed a hint of shyness as she gestured downward.

'I hope I'm dressed OK? I wasn't sure where we're going.'

A sensation suspiciously akin to panic roiled in his gut. Why on earth had this seemed a good idea?

'For a picnic,' he muttered. *Muttered?* 'A picnic,' he repeated firmly. 'I thought that would be more private.'

Her expression registered a panic that no doubt mirrored his own. 'Private?'

'So that no one will be able to overhear our conversation,' he added hurriedly. 'Plus, yesterday you saw a lot of urban Lycander. I thought you might like to see somewhere more tranquil.'

In addition, he'd hoped a sylvan setting would influence her, that his words would be more persuasive in a less official ambiance.

'We're going to eat in the royal forest. I've arranged for the food to be delivered. It was a bit short notice, so it won't be anything fancy, I'm afraid, but...'

As silence greeted this, it belatedly occurred to Marcus that the idea that had seemed brilliant in the confines of his office that morning no longer seemed quite so stellar.

Perhaps he should have wined and dined her in style? Perhaps a charm offensive would have dazzled her and impressed her into compliance? Unfortunately charm wasn't his bag—was not a tool of his trade.

Even as a child he'd lacked charm. Charm would have got him nowhere with his parents—would have made no difference to their levels of violence or indifference, depending on their alcohol consumption or their reaction to the drug of the day. Charm certainly wouldn't have helped him on the tough streets of his childhood, where sheer brute strength and the ability to fight dirty had been the only currency worth a dime. And by the time of his adoption it had all been too late—charm had quite simply never come into play. So it was unrealistic to expect it to come to his aid now. As for the picnic... He must have been running mad.

'Of course if you would prefer we could simply divert to my office and...'

But then she smiled and his words dried up.

'No. Sorry, you took me by surprise. A picnic sounds lovely, and it does seem the best way to make sure our conversation remains between us.'

'OK. Great.'

The car pulled into the small car park, and as they climbed out Marcus's phone rang.

'Hi, Marcus. I've got the picnic and I've brought it to Umbrella Copse.'

'Thank you, Gloria. We'll be right there.'

Perhaps this would work out after all. He could see April's appreciation as she tipped her head upwards to catch the dappled rays of the sun that filtered through the luxuriant trees, flecking the vibrant greens with droplets of gold. For an instant his gaze lingered on the elegant length of her neck, then moved over the beauty of her face, the smattering of freckles on the bridge of her nose, the...

Stop and focus.

The point was that the lazy drone of bees, the call of the black kites, all seemed to indicate the need for tranquility and concord. Which would hopefully aid him in his quest—the reason he was here. To ensure that April dropped her story.

Then they reached the glade and Marcus came to an abrupt halt as he took in the scene before him.

For a long moment words failed him.

A wooden slatted picnic table was covered in a snow-white tablecloth, and laid with gleaming silver cutlery, fluted crystal glasses and bone china plates. A bottle of Lycander's best Sauvignon Blanc nestled in a state-of-the-art cooler. A wicker picnic basket was on the bench, and Gloria was busy unpacking an array of delicacies onto large china platters.

She turned and beamed at him. 'Perfect timing,' she declared.

Marcus attempted to regroup as he mentally

replayed his earlier conversation with Gloria in his head.

'Hi Gloria. Could I ask a favour? Would you be able to rustle up a picnic for two—nothing fancy?'

Now he said, 'Gloria—this is...amazing. But you shouldn't have gone to so much trouble. I wasn't expecting anything like this.'

'It is no trouble.' The dark-haired woman turned to April. 'In all the time I have worked with him not once has he asked for a picnic, and not once has he asked us to create a meal for him and a lady—so we decided to make this special.'

Marcus opened his mouth to explain that this was a strictly business lunch and then closed it again. Gloria had gone to a great deal of trouble and, however low on charm he was, he wouldn't hurt her feelings.

'It's fabulous, Gloria. Thank you—and please thank everyone in the kitchens as well.'

'Of course.' Gloria arranged a centrepiece posy of freshly picked flowers—a glorious burst of red, orange and yellow blooms—and smiled with satisfaction. 'Enjoy.'

'Please add my thanks as well,' April said, and

her voice was full of appreciation but underlaid with a tinge of panic he recognised all too well.

'You're very welcome. Enjoy.' A beaming smile, a nod, and Gloria was gone.

Swallowing the urge to call her back—after all that would be cowardly in the extreme—Marcus looked at April, then at the picnic, and then back at April.

'Um…'

Forget charm—even the art of conversation had deserted him, and a miasma of awkwardness descended. It seemed clear that April had been thrown a curve ball too—her cool self-containment looked more than a little fragmented.

And then, to his surprise, she gave a small chuckle—a sound that seemed to surprise her as much as it did him.

'Your face!' she said. 'You looked absolutely horrified. Though I have to admit you covered it beautifully.'

He couldn't help it; her smile transformed her face, lightened it in a way he couldn't fully explain, and the sight caused his own lips to upturn. 'I really am sorry. I didn't want to make you feel awkward. It didn't cross my mind Gloria would think this was a date.'

'Because you don't *ever* date?'

'I really don't.'

Not his thing. The closeness, the questions, the intimacy of a date was not to his liking. Every so often there was a woman—he didn't embrace celibacy—but if pushed to describe his relationships the adjectives that came to mind were 'brief', 'clean' and 'functional'. 'Relationship' was too deep a word—they were more like understandings, interludes, soon over and forgotten, conducted discreetly and anonymously, outside of Lycander.

'I can't really see the point.'

Her eyebrows arched. 'Most people would disagree. It's a chance to get to know someone, work out if you're compatible...'

'I don't need to have dinner with someone to work out compatibility.'

Pink tinged her cheeks and suddenly awareness swept in on the summer breeze, heightening his senses, illuminating the green of the leaves, the glitter of the cutlery in the sunshine, and urging him to step forward and show her exactly how well matched he knew *they* would be.

She hauled in an audible breath. 'I wasn't talking about physical compatibility. I meant…overall compatibility—whether you actually *like* the other person, have something in common with them.'

'Nope—still not relevant.'

'So you are only interested in the physical side of things?'

'Yes.'

'At least you're honest.'

Was it his imagination or did she actually look intrigued rather than critical or outraged? Belatedly his radar kicked in. April was a reporter—of *course* she was intrigued. She was probably converting his words into some sort of headline right now. *Lycander's Lothario says, 'Let's get physical!'*

Note to whatever brain cells he had left: *this woman is an adversary.*

'Yes.' He gestured to the table. 'Anyway, we seem to be off track. Now we've established that this isn't a date I think we should get started.'

'Agreed.'

But to his escalating annoyance it wasn't as easy as all that. Even as he busied himself with the pouring of wine, the choice of food, he knew the simple movements were overhung with an insidious curiosity as to what it would be like if this *were* a date. Would they clink their glasses in a toast to each other? Accidentally entangle their feet under the table? Pop morsels of food into each other's mouths?

For an instant his gaze lingered on the lushness of her lips and he wondered if he was losing his grasp on sanity. Not once in his life had he felt the temptation to feed a woman a morsel of pâté on sourdough bread, and he sure as heck wasn't starting now.

Time to get back on track and recall that this was emphatically *not* a date, or anything resembling it. It was a negotiation table. 'So. To business. I'll keep it simple. Will you drop the story?'

Her body tensed as if in acknowledgment of the fact that they were now down to brass tacks—that the interlude, whatever it had meant, was over.

'It's not that straightforward.'

'Yes, it is. Frederick is a good ruler and he

needs time—he needs to be given a chance, exactly as the majority of those teenagers you met yesterday believe.'

'They also said they would only believe in the monarchy if it wasn't founded on a lie.' April shook her head, looked down at her plate and spread more pâté onto a slice of bread, as if to distract herself. 'But if what Brian Sewell told me is true then Frederick's ascent to the throne *is* based on a lie. So I have a solution. I'll tell you what he said, and if you tell me he is lying I'll drop the story.'

April sipped her wine and then met his gaze full-on. Her directness brooked no quarter.

'Frederick should have been in the car the night Axel died. He bailed out from that function to go and party and Axel took his place—even though Axel pretended it was all his idea.'

She paused as she studied his face, and he focused on maintaining an expression of calm interest.

'Is that true?'

'I'll take the Fifth.'

'So it *is* true?'

'I didn't say that. But what I *will* say is that even

if it were true, hypothetically speaking, it wouldn't matter.'

'The truth *always* matters.' Her voice was absolute in its conviction. 'The bottom line is that Frederick chose pleasure over duty and his brother paid with his life. The people deserve to know that.'

'Why?'

'Because if he lied to them once he could lie to them again.'

Time to change tack. 'For a start, the truth isn't that black and white, cut and dried—whatever cliché you like. Frederick *did* attend a party the night of Axel's death. But it was a business function to celebrate a business deal—not some wild celebrity shindig. Frederick founded Freddy Petrelli's Olive Oil, and the deal took his company into the global arena. *Axel* was heir to the throne—Frederick had no interest in politics at the time. So I'm not sure your "pleasure over duty" theme will hold water.'

'Then what is all the fuss about? Why would it have been covered up in the first place?'

'Because Axel was Lycander's hope for the future—the Golden Prince who would take Lycander back to prosperity and fairness. At the time Frederick was pretty unpopular—he was seen as being like his father because of his party lifestyle. Bottom line is that the people would have *preferred* Frederick to have been in that car, and they loathed the idea that *he* was now heir to the throne. The throne was already rocking; if they had known he should have been in the car the monarchy could have been overturned.'

'So, hypothetically speaking, you agree that a cover-up was the right way to go?'

'It is what Axel would have wanted. Whatever it took for his vision of Lycander to be achieved and for the monarchy he believed in to remain stable.'

That was what had driven Marcus to step forward to offer Frederick his support, even when his own grief was at its height.

'He believed in Frederick.'

'That isn't the point. The point is that by concealing the truth Frederick may have changed history—changed people's lives.'

'For the better.'

'Maybe, but maybe not. And maybe not long-term. And—'

'You can play alternative endings until you're rainbow-coloured, but at the end of the day you make the decision you make on the day.'

'And what if it turns out to be the wrong one?'

'Then you have to live with the consequences.'

The words came out way too harsh as memory stirred, pulling him back to eighteen years before, and the decision he'd made then. He'd rescued Elvira from the fire and had made the decision not to go back in for his parents.

Little matter that, given the state of the fire, he would most likely not have survived. Little matter that he had been restrained by his neighbours. He knew that if Elvira had still been inside somehow he would have broken free and tried to save her—would have perished in the attempt. But he hadn't done so for his parents. A decision made that he had to live with. And God have mercy on his soul.

He pulled his mind from his own thoughts and flinched at the expression on April's face. The colour had leeched from her face and despite her best efforts to cover it up her hand shook as she placed her glass down. Wine slopped over the side and spread a puddle on the white of the table-cloth.

'April...?' In that second he knew with bone-deep certainty that whatever demons haunted April, whatever decisions she rued in her life, they rivalled his own. 'I'm sorry.'

'No. *I'm* sorry.' She reached for a napkin, fumbled, and hauled in an audible breath. 'I'm fine.'

'No. You aren't.'

He could sense the pain that emanated from her and wanted to soothe it. Lord knew he could empathise with the whip of guilt and pain. Without thought he reached out and covered her hand in his, and felt sensation jolt his veins and heat his blood. Her green eyes widened, as if her reaction to his touch had jerked her from the edge of pain.

'Then I *will* be fine.'

Her gaze lingered on his hand and gently she pulled her own out from under it, retrieved the napkin and scrubbed at the wine stain.

'But there is something I want to know. You told me how the *people* felt about Frederick and Axel. What about *you*? Axel was your best friend. How did *you* feel?'

Marcus closed his eyes in an attempt to ward

the question off; this was something he had spoken to no one about—not even Elvira. But suddenly here and now, as he opened his eyes, met her gaze and saw the genuine compassion in them, for a moment he wanted to share the grief.

Axel had been like a brother to him—the one person he had let a little close. They had been best friends as boys, had run and played together, argued politics and crafted Lycander's future together. But...

'My feelings are irrelevant. It is Lycander that matters. Nothing can bring Axel back. His death was a tragedy, but maybe his legacy can live on.'

April nodded, her green eyes wide with empathy as well as sympathy. 'I am sorry for your loss,' she said simply, 'and I appreciate how strongly you believe that Frederick is the right person to rule Lycander now. And I do understand why you want me to drop the story.'

'Will you?'

'I don't know. I'm not sure it is up to me to make a decision of such enormity with such huge possible repercussions. I need to think.'

'Understood.'

There would be no point in pushing her and in truth he understood her stance.

'So, right now why don't you have some of Gloria's chocolate and apple torte, famed throughout the region? And then I'll drop you back to your hotel.'

She nodded slowly. 'Thank you.'

But as they ate the sumptuously decadent dessert conversation dwindled, both of them caught up in their own thoughts, both of them with decisions to make.

Marcus glanced at the serious intent on April's face as she dabbed up the last flakes of pastry with one finger. He didn't know which way her choice would fall—he suspected neither did she.

A sylvan picnic hadn't cut the mustard, nor even the Lycander tomato chutney, so he needed to move to Plan B.

CHAPTER FIVE

APRIL OPENED HER eyes and puffed out a sigh.
She might as well face it—sleep had left the hotel
room and it wasn't coming back. Unless her fit-
ful, restless swivel round the sheets counted.

Every time she closed her eyes Marcus Alrikson—drat the man—insisted on an invasion of
her dreams. As she lay there, gazing wide-eyed
at the ceiling, irritation and a dollop of sheer guilt
swathed her already heated skin and she pushed
the duvet off with more force than necessary.

This was unacceptable. This unwanted attraction had caused her to lose the thing she valued
most—her objectivity. She couldn't see her way
forward—couldn't work out what to do about the
story she almost wished she'd never discovered.
Part of her wanted to drop it. Problem was, she
couldn't be sure of her motivation. Had she allowed her attraction for him to cloud her judgement and make her want to do what he said?

Her entire being revolted against the very concept that she would be foolish enough to do that again. Attraction had rendered her unable to see Dean as he truly was—had propelled her into a foolish, disastrous and tragic marriage.

April wanted to pull the duvet over her head and go into hibernation mode... *No way.* That way lay the path back to depression. Right now she needed to kill this attraction off, shut her hormones down and focus on a return to her safe, even-keeled life—the one she had worked so hard to construct, brick by painstaking brick.

The buzz of her phone provided a welcome relief from her thoughts.

'Hey, Kathy.' Her editor, who could perhaps help with this dilemma. Except she wasn't sure she wanted the decision taken out of her hands...

'April. Glad I caught you. I've just spoken with Marcus Alrikson and it sounds like you've ruffled some feathers.'

For a moment words deserted her as the sheer gall of the man blasted her. But it wasn't only anger—there was a sense of betrayal as well. He'd gone over her head to her editor.

'I really don't know what you were *thinking,*

April. We were very lucky to get this exclusive coverage of the Lycander Royal wedding, and we agreed to write a feel-good article on the lifestyle of the royal couple—not to dig up a political scandal. You have single-handedly nearly screwed that up.'

The tone of the other woman's voice twanged a nerve—a reminder of the numerous occasions on which Dean and his family had explained to April why she didn't measure up. As a wife, a mother, a person... The memory kept her vocal cords in stranglehold, conveying an almost hypnotic belief that, yes, she *was* wrong, stupid...

April dug her nails into the palm of her hand to wake herself up. Tragedy had reformed her and she was no longer that woman. 'Kathy,' she broke in, 'this is not just a scandal. It's a political story that could have huge ramifications if it's true.'

'Perhaps, but it is not the sort of story our readers would be interested in. Marcus Alrikson has made it plain that if we don't back off they back *out*—and the wedding coverage will go to *What's Up?* instead. I will not lose this to our biggest competitor. So drop the story.'

'But—' April began, feeling conflicting emotions tear at her. Relief that the decision had been taken out of her hands versus her principles, which told her that the decision was hers to make, and had to be made on different grounds than readership numbers.

'No buts. Drop the story. I had an agreement with Marcus Alrikson—I intend to keep it.'

Five minutes later April flung her phone onto the bed. In record time she shed her tartan PJs, tugged on jeans and a dark blue T-shirt, grabbed her bag and blazer and left her hotel room. How *dared* he? Of all the arrogant, idiotic—

Her mental invective halted as she strode through the lobby, out through the revolving doors and glared around for a taxi.

Once at Marcus's offices she didn't even pause—she stormed inside with no more than a perfunctory glance at the historic grandeur of the building. Right now she didn't care if he was in Fort bloody Knox—she'd find him. And if he wasn't in she'd wait for as long as it took.

Attempting to summon a polite smile, she approached the semi-circular reception desk. 'Is Marcus Alrikson available?'

'Ah, you must be April. I'm Karen. Marcus

asked me to take you straight up when you arrived.'

'He did?' A tiny puff of wind left her sails of fury, but April soon remedied that as adrenalin pulsed through her. If he was willing to fight, then bring it on. 'Excellent.'

She followed the petite blonde receptionist down a maze of corridors and up a flight of oak-banister stairs—the building appeared to have been haphazardly converted from royal residence to office complex.

'Is Marcus expecting me at a certain time?'

The woman nodded. 'He said somewhere between nine-thirty and ten-thirty.'

So she was *that* predictable, was she?

April caught a glimpse of her reflection in a gilded mirror. Her eyes had squinted to slits and her expression defined the word *glower*, so she couldn't blame Karen for her apprehensive glance.

Finally they reached a door where a discreet plaque showed they'd reached their destination. A perfunctory knock, then Karen announced April's name in a relieved murmur and scurried back down the corridor.

Marcus rose from behind a teak desk that screeched antiquity. 'April. I'm guessing you've spoken with Kathy.'

'Yes, I have, and I am here to tell you that you are *despicable*. You went over my head and behind my back to my editor. I could have been sacked.'

'Rubbish!' But a tinge of discomfort climbed his cheeks. 'I explained that you had strayed from the brief, but I also made it crystal-clear that you were doing a fantastic job on the wedding article and that I categorically wanted you to continue with that.'

April could hear the hiss of metaphorical steam from her ears. 'So now you want my *thanks*?'

'No.' All signs of unease had vanished. 'I simply want you to get on with the agreed article.'

'I am. But I have come across a separate story about Axel and I have told you I need time to consider what to do about it.'

'And that's what you now have. Time. Write the article on the wedding. At the end of that, if you want to pursue the other story you can. There will be nothing I can do about it. But I want to make sure you do really consider the consequences.'

He moved away from the desk, his frustration evident in each stride. 'I am not asking you to cover up a crime. Even if Brian Sewell is telling the truth, Frederick did nothing wrong; the events of that night were simply a tragedy. One we all have to live with and make the best of.'

The words smote her—extinguished her anger in an ice-cold deluge. She knew oh-so-well how a few minutes could change your entire world. How one decision could have a domino effect you had never intended. But did that make you any less guilty…? April didn't think so. In which case Frederick should have to face up to what he'd done.

Yet *she* hadn't, had she? What jury had judged *her*? What punishment had *she* received apart from the life sentence of having to live each and every day without Edward, imagining how it might have been? He would have been six years old. Six years and few months. He'd be at school… He'd…

Stop. That way led nowhere. The clock couldn't be turned back. Perhaps Frederick wished it could be.

Think.

Hard to do that when once again her body was hyper-alert to the man now standing so tantalisingly close to her. For a moment of insanity she wanted to close the gap between them and throw herself at the bulk of him, lose herself, submerge these roiling thoughts in desire. After all, he had said it himself—his only interest in women was on a physical level. And for years and years April hadn't felt so much as a semi-spark, a micro-spark of desire for any man.

Get. A. Grip. Think. Objectively.

Marcus met her gaze full-on. 'I believe it is in Lycander's best interests for this story not to be pursued. You also have my personal word that Frederick has done nothing wrong.'

'Your "personal word" is simply an expression of your personal opinion. Many others may not agree. Plus, it's hard to put much stock in your word.'

Now anger flashed across his face and instinctively she stepped back; fear could still surface after all these years.

His expression morphed into a frown at her involuntary reaction and she forced herself to continue. 'Going to Kathy was hardly above-board.'

'I did what I needed to do.'

There was no compromise in his tone, and again she braced herself, waiting for the tide of anger, the bluster, the threats.

Instead he said, 'I won't apologise for that. But I *am* sorry if there was negative fallout for you. I did my best to minimise that.'

For a second she had the feeling that he had surprised himself. Dammit, she almost felt *grateful*—and that made her even more furious. True, he could have requested she be kicked off the story altogether, but she had still been manipulated and she hated it—it was too reminiscent of her time with Dean, and she would not take it.

But what could she do? Tell Marcus to stuff it? Resign from the wedding article and pursue the other story? The problem with that was that it smacked of cutting her nose off to spite her face. For a start it would be professional idiocy and, truth be told, she still wasn't sure she even wanted to pursue the story.

What to do? What to do?

Objectivity still eluded her. Not even a particle of it was to be found as she tried to think. Her story had the power to be the catalyst to topple a throne—and she *did* need time to decide what to do with it. But, dammit, she wouldn't just sit back and be manipulated.

'So you've guaranteed that I take time to consider? Fine. But I need something more than time.'

'Such as?'

Suspicion tinged his voice and her anger resurfaced as he assumed the reason.

'I won't be blackmailed.'

The anger swelled, rolled words off her tongue. 'If you want me to take your word for it that pursuing this story is the morally wrong thing to do, then prove it. Let me shadow you—let me see what Lycander is all about. Show me what Frederick is doing. More than the community centre.'

She took a deep breath. She'd show him *blackmail*.

'And I want an exclusive article with *you*. We could call it *The Real Marcus Alrikson*. On the record.'

Even as she said the words she felt an unholy glee at the knowledge that this would be his worst nightmare.

For a second, sheer horror etched his face. 'Forget it. I told you—I won't be blackmailed.'

'It's not blackmail. It's a means to help me make a decision and a way for me to retrieve my reputation with Kathy.'

There was a long silence as he gazed past her, clearly deep in thought. His fingers drummed the desk in an impatient tattoo and then ceased as he looked at her.

For an instant she thought he'd call her bluff, but then he nodded. 'OK. But I get to vet the finished product.'

'We can *discuss* the finished product,' she conceded even as she frowned. Had that been too easy? Why on earth had he capitulated? 'But that doesn't mean you get to rewrite it, and when I interview you it will be *on* the record. You get that, right?'

'Sure,' he said easily—and as she looked into those dark eyes she knew damn well that he had no intent of letting her anywhere *near* the real him. Well, they would see...

Curiosity, determination and a funny little thrill shot through her. 'So, when do we start?'

'No time like the present. I have meetings

scheduled this morning on education, on overseas aid, and a general security briefing. I'll need to talk to Frederick and get this cleared. Then, tonight, we'll attend a charity ball.'

'A charity ball?'

Insidious panic touched her. The entire concept of attendance at any glitterati function as a guest filled her with acute anxiety. Too overwhelming—too much. Since Edward's death she had avoided social occasions as if they truly could give her the plague—the thought of making conversation was too much.

'Yes. It's an annual event, hosted by Rafael Martinez and his wife—'

'Cora Derwent,' April completed. 'Lady Kaitlin Derwent's twin sister. The same Lady Kaitlin who was once linked with Prince Frederick.'

'That's the one.' Marcus picked up his phone. 'I'll call now and explain that I'll be taking up my plus one option.'

'I... I don't have anything to wear.'

His look indicated that he felt she might have lost the plot. 'You are in a shopper's paradise, April. That won't be a problem.'

'Of course.' Seeing his look of puzzlement, she forced a smile. 'I'll hit the shops at lunchtime.'

For heaven's sake, she should be *pleased*—she would be attending a function where celebrities would abound, and most importantly she'd won an exclusive scoop—the chance to shadow Marcus Alrikson for four days.

The words encircled her brain. *Shadow Marcus Alrikson for four days.*

Suddenly the sense of victory was hollow in her tummy. What on earth had made her believe this was a good idea?

'Why is this a good idea?'

Prince Frederick sat behind the ornate antique desk in the Lycander throne room, a look of genuine bewilderment on his face.

Marcus sat opposite him and did his best to maintain an expression of being totally in control of the situation.

'Let me get this straight,' Frederick continued, one blond eyebrow raised in question. 'You have agreed to let April Fotherington shadow you for four days, including council meetings, and she is going to write an article on "the real Marcus Alrikson" as well as the wedding article?'

'Yes.'

'I don't get it.' Frederick shook his head. 'I mean, I understand you don't want April to pursue the other story, but this doesn't sound like the usual ruthless Alrikson approach.'

'Sometimes the ruthless approach isn't the best option.' Even to himself the words sounded lame. 'I decided this was the best way to head off the threat.'

Yup. More and more lame.

The royal eyebrow rose further. 'But at the end of the four days April might still pursue the story?'

Marcus nodded, wondering how to explain something he didn't understand himself. 'I realise that. But...'

Somehow he wanted April to *choose* to drop the story. He resisted the urge to close his eyes in sheer frustration with himself, and gathered himself together.

'In the next four days I will close Brian Sewell down. We are close to getting the evidence we need to nail him. Once he is discredited, her story will have no foundation. I'll also uncover any other potential sources.'

Frederick frowned, his blue eyes shadowed. 'Perhaps she's right. Perhaps I *should* simply tell the truth.'

'It isn't that easy,' Marcus said. 'And we both know the time isn't right.'

Frederick exhaled a sigh and bowed his head in acknowledgment before his lips turned up in a sudden impish smile. 'Well, I will look forward to reading all about "the real Marcus Alrikson".' He shrugged. 'Though I still haven't grasped why you agreed to that either.'

Who knew? Unfortunately Marcus had a sneaking suspicion that it was to do with his impulsive regret that he'd gone over April's head to her editor—got her into trouble, betrayed her. Still…

'I have no intention of giving her any interesting material, so I doubt the article will see the light of day.'

Frederick's smile increased in size to accommodate his patent disbelief, but to Marcus's relief he refrained from comment.

'Keep me posted,' was all he said.

Marcus nodded. 'I'll see you later at the council meeting.' *With a certain reporter in tow...*

Two and a half hours and two meetings later Marcus watched as his colleagues filed out of the room, then turned to look at April.

Although he had forced himself to focus on the agenda, he'd found his gaze inexorably pulled towards her, where she'd sat quietly, her expression intent as she unobtrusively took copious notes.

'What did you think?' he asked.

'It was fascinating. I've never had the opportunity to be part of something like this. I loved it. And I was impressed—Frederick does really care, and so do you. About education and about how Lycander can play a part in the world.'

'Education is central to the future, and we also owe a debt to the children who grew up in Alphonse's reign, who have been let down by the system for years. Those teenagers, young adults, adults who didn't get any education, who learnt their life lessons on the streets. I don't want them to be forgotten.' *The people he and Elvira could have become.* 'I want them to be given choices and opportunities.'

'Do you think it's too late for some of them?'

'I don't know. But I know we have to try. Some of those people are the next generation; we need the teens of today to believe that the system that let them down has changed. That's why we must crack down on crime and apathy and poverty. The whole sorry cycle.' He shrugged. 'I'm sorry. You've had three hours of policy. I won't bore you further.'

'I'm not bored at all. How can something so important be tedious?'

Her expression showed genuine sincerity, and when he remembered her true interest in the community centre he couldn't help but ask, 'Have you never thought of moving on from celebrity interviews to more serious articles?'

It was as if he'd pulled a plug—his words doused her light of enthusiasm utterly.

'No. I've found my niche and I'm happy there.'

'Why?'

'I enjoy what I do and I don't want the hassle of starting again. I was lucky to get this job and I'm in a good place. I don't want to rock the boat.'

Ever. He could almost hear the unspoken word. 'So you want your life to remain exactly as it is?'

'Yes.' April tilted her chin in a gesture that stated defiance, yet he noted she'd folded her arms as if in self-defence. 'What's wrong with that?'

'You're not even thirty. Surely you have career aspirations? And presumably one day you want a family?'

'Nope.' The word held an almost bleak finality, and as if she'd realised she hurried on. 'I've met all my aspirations. I don't need any more. My life is where I need it to be. I don't ask for or want more.' She closed her notebook with an emphatic *thunk*. 'Right. I'm off to the shops.'

The topic of her future was clearly closed and padlocked, but that didn't stop the questions in Marcus's head. April was young, beautiful, intelligent, and interested in way more than celebrity chit-chat—so why on earth didn't she want more? And had she really vetoed having a family? That didn't make sense.

Or maybe it did. After all, he was thirty and he'd done exactly that.

Not, he reminded himself, that April's life goals mattered to *him*. Except in so far as an understanding of them might make it easier for him to persuade her to drop the story about the night of Axel's death. He just didn't like to see her sell herself short…

Not your business.

'Actually, I can help out there,' he said. 'Sunita has recommended a boutique.' He glanced at his watch. 'I'll take you there now.'

An expression he couldn't interpret crossed her face.

'Is that a problem?'

'I'm quite capable of shopping by myself. There is no need to come with me.'

'I couldn't agree more, but Sunita asked me to—apparently people have taken to going into boutiques pretending they have been sent by her in the hope of getting a discount. I need to come along to vouch for you.'

'Oh.'

Marcus frowned. He couldn't help but wonder what train her thoughts had climbed aboard.

'Then…um…thank you.'

'No problem. Let's go. We can walk from here. It's called Fashion Plate.'

The short journey was achieved in silence. Marcus could sense the discomfort emanating from

April, as if she were heading out to do something she found almost distasteful. It seemed clear that her claim to dislike shopping was genuine.

Though she *did* stop as they approached the shop in order to study the window display—four mannequins of different race, hair colour, height and build had been posed as if they were marching around a plate-shaped display of accessories—shoes, bags and even tiaras.

As they pushed the shop door open to the sound of a small discreet chime, a woman headed straight for them. Svelte and elegant, she epitomised *chic*, and her smile was the perfect blend of welcome and discretion.

'Welcome to Fashion Plate.' Her eyes widened slightly as she looked at Marcus. 'I am Gabrielle. *You* are Marcus Alrikson and this must be April. Your PA contacted me, and of course we are most happy to help.' Her eyes swept over April and she nodded. 'We have set aside some time for a fitting, and of course to discuss what you are looking for. I understand you need a dress for the Martinez Charity Ball?'

'Yes.'

April had tensed beside him, her expression less than enthused, though her tone was polite.

'But there is absolutely no need for a fitting as I am pushed for time. I am quite happy to simply browse and find a dress myself.'

Gabrielle looked horrified. 'No, no. I wouldn't hear of it.' Her expert eye travelled over April again. 'You and Mr Alrikson will be given refreshments in our private room, and I will find a selection of dresses for you to look at. You are a friend of Sunita and I insist.'

'Um...' April hesitated and then, with a fulminating stare at Marcus—for all the world as though this were *his* fault—followed Gabrielle through the shop.

Minutes later they had been seated in a small but cleverly furnished boudoir-like room. The walls held a selection of black and white photographs from different eras of fashion, as well as large mirrors that created a feeling of space. Another assistant served them tea in exquisite china cups, along with a plate of melt-in-the-mouth biscuits.

April waited until the assistant had left, and then glared at Marcus. 'Well, thanks for the help.'

'What did you expect me to do? Acquiescence seemed to be the quickest way forward.' He smiled. 'You're lucky *I* came with you and not Sunita—believe me, she would have insisted you go the whole nine yards with the fitting. The only reason she didn't come is that Amil isn't very well, and whilst Sunita may love clothes she loves Amil more.'

For a second he thought April flinched, and in a movement so swift he barely noticed she squeezed her hand into a fist, almost as if she were pushing her nails into her palm, and then she relaxed her hand again.

'As she should—he is her son. But you're right. This *would* have been even worse if she were here. Sunita and I have a differing view on clothes. For her, they are a vocation. She is a mine of knowledge and expertise on all aspects—the design, the feel, the material, the costs, the labour. She feels real passion for clothes.'

'And for you?'

'They are functional.' Picking up a biscuit, she took a small bite and huffed out a sigh. 'Anyway, whilst we are stuck in here we may as well use the time. What's *your* take on clothes?'

'Same as yours. They are functional.'

April waited, then made a 'come on' gesture with her hands. 'Could you expand on that?'

'Not really. There isn't much else to say.'

'Let's try it a different way. This morning you got up and at some point changed out of your PJs into your clothes.'

'Actually, I don't wear pyjamas.'

April closed her eyes, a tantalising hint of pink climbing her cheekbones, and Marcus couldn't help himself.

'Not even so much as a pair of tightie-whities. The technical term I think is "commando". In other words stark boll—'

Her eyes sprang open. 'I get it. Thank you. Vividly. I'm sure my readers will appreciate the detail,' she added.

Damn. That victory had been short-lived— the idea of Lycander's population imagining the Prince's Chief Advisor going commando did *not* fill him with joy.

'*Touché,*' he acknowledged.

'So you dressed in jeans and a T-shirt. Why?'

'Comfort. We decided a couple of years ago to drop the need for suits or formal clothing during council meetings. We knew the meetings could be time-consuming and sometimes stressful. Comfort seemed a priority.'

'Was it your idea?'

'Yes.'

April surveyed him for a moment, her head tilted to one side. 'But there was another reason, wasn't there?'

Damn, she was good at reading people. 'Of course not.'

With a sigh, she put down her pen. 'Off the record?'

'OK. Fine. I suggested it because I thought it would give Frederick *more* authority rather than less. I thought it would make him more human and indicate to the council that he was open to new ideas and not an autocrat like his father.'

'So you believe that clothes can be useful?'

'Yes.'

In his childhood, clothes had been a sorry affair—unwashed, ill-fitting and scruffy. Until that magical day when his parents had inadvertently let him see a stash of goods 'off the back of a lorry' and he had taken a pair of designer trainers. They had been livid, but he hadn't cared.

Those trainers had shown him the power that could be wielded by clothes—the kudos he'd gained from street kids who wouldn't usually look at him had been an eye-opener.

'People judge you by your clothes, and you can use that to your own advantage. You shouldn't judge a book by its cover, but most people do.'

'That can be a monumental mistake.'

'It's still a fact. Clothes send a message, and as such they are a tool to be used.'

'Is that what you do? You personally? Do you dress for other people?'

'No. I dress for myself. But if an expensive suit will prove a point to whoever I am sitting across a negotiating table from then I may choose to wear it. The image you project can matter in some situations.'

Before she could respond, there was a knock on the door and Gabrielle entered with three dresses draped over her arm. In a deft movement she hung two up on a rail by the door and held up the remaining one.

'I think this is the one.'

Marcus glanced at the dress. His knowledge of fashion wasn't up to much, but he registered an impression of red, stripes and lace. Turning to see April's reaction, he clocked her panic before she shook her head in a firm rejection.

'It's beautiful, Gabrielle, but it isn't me. It's too obvious. I'm a writer—an observer. I don't want to be noticed.'

The words made a level of sense—indeed, they echoed the view he had just put forward about the importance of clothes—so perhaps he had misinterpreted the panic. And yet...

'Surely tonight it doesn't matter? After all I am your subject and I know you're observing me already, so please don't hold back on my account.'

Perhaps his motivation was selfish—he knew she would look incredible in the dress and he wanted to see her in it.

'I would still prefer to be less visible rather than more. This event will be star-studded—I'd like to observe the guests without being noticed.'

Gabrielle waved away the objection. 'At an event like this one you will stand out if you do *not* wear something like this. There will be nothing that will mark you out more clearly as an observer than wearing a dull black dress that conceals your assets rather than showcasing them.'

Her gaze swept again over April's current outfit of jeans, T-shirt and blazer, and although she was way too professional to shudder, Marcus felt it was a close-run thing.

It was clear that Gabrielle's argument had temporarily stymied April, and Marcus settled back on the small spindle-legged chair to observe the action.

Gabrielle continued with enthusiasm. 'Take this opportunity. Tonight you will be noticed no matter what; you will arrive on the arm of Marcus Alrikson, and no matter what capacity that is in people will be looking at you. So...this dress... it is a necessity.'

April paled, and now there could be no mistake—for some reason Gabrielle's words had left her stricken, and without thought Marcus rose to his feet, his amusement routed by concern and an instinct to protect her. For some unfathomable reason the idea of wearing this dress clearly had April in a state...

'We appreciate all the help. But I think it would be best if you could find April a simple black dress, or whatever it is April wants. After all Sunita always tells me it is important that a person feels comfortable in her skin as well as in her dress.'

The mention of Sunita did the trick. 'Of course.' Gabrielle hesitated, then turned to April. 'I apologise if I overstepped—but you are a beautiful woman and it is my instinct to want to show that to the world.'

April managed a smile. 'Thank you. That is a generous thing to say—and please don't feel you've overstepped. I am just not very good with clothes.'

Once Gabrielle had left she turned to Marcus. 'Thank you.'

'No problem.' He gestured towards the dresses. 'If you don't like them then you don't like them. That's your prerogative. You should wear whatever you want to wear.'

'And it doesn't bother you?'

Her question held an element of timidity that seemed totally out of character.

'No. Why should it?'

'Because... Well, it's occurred to me that Gabrielle is right. All eyes are going to be on us. You never take a plus-one to events like this, and you don't ever give interviews.'

He shrugged. 'I have no problem with people looking at us.'

'And you have no problem with me wearing whatever I choose to wear?'

'No.' He had absolutely zip idea where she was going with this.

For a long moment she studied his expression, and a small sweet smile tipped her lips. 'You mean that, don't you?'

'Of course I do.' Marcus frowned. 'Are you worried about what *I* choose to wear?'

'Of course not. You can come in your pyjamas for all I care—' She broke off, a ludicrous look of dismay on her face. 'If you had any, I mean… though… I mean… Well…obviously I'd prefer you to be wearing *something.*' Suddenly she giggled. 'Though if you weren't I guess at least no one would be looking at *me.* Whatever I wear.'

Her laughter was clear, melodious and infectious, and he couldn't help but join in. Then somehow the whole conversation, her sheer beauty, and their shared laughter prompted a change in the atmosphere and their mirth subsided.

They stared at each other and then he stepped forward, reducing the gap between them. She followed suit. Now they were so close he could count the smattering of faint freckles on the bridge of her nose.

'April...?'

But before she could answer there was a knock on the door. April jumped backwards and turned away from him as Gabrielle re-entered.

She looked from one to the other but said nothing. 'I have found this,' she announced, holding up a long black dress, her nose slightly wrinkled in disapproval.

'Thank you. I'll try it on.' Without looking at Marcus, April said, 'Do you mind waiting outside?'

'No problem.'

Right now fresh air was exactly what he needed—that or a long cold shower, or a brisk run.

Ten minutes later April emerged from the shop, a bag held loosely in her hand.

'Successful?' he asked.

She glanced down at the bag and then back to him. 'Time will tell.'

CHAPTER SIX

APRIL SURVEYED HER reflection in the hotel room's mirror and wondered if she had perhaps run a little mad, even lifting a hand to her forehead to check her temperature.

What had possessed her? What *still* possessed her?

She had no idea.

But as she'd stood in that room with Gabrielle she had looked at the black dress and then at the other one.

Gabrielle had given a small Gallic shrug. 'It matters not which dress you wear. He will not take his eyes from you. That is plain.'

April shook her head. 'It's not like that. I am writing an article on him. That's all.'

Gabrielle had given her a look of polite disbelief but said nothing as April had continued to look at both dresses.

Then, 'Perhaps I *will* try it on. The first one.'

'*Bon!* Good!'

Gabrielle had ushered her into the fitting room and minutes later April had stared at her reflection. The same reflection she stared at now. Of a woman she barely recognised. With the emphasis on 'barely'. The dress was strapless, showing off her shoulders and arms, discreetly tantalising with a hint of cleavage. The nude underlay was covered by a layer of red lace and a bold swathe of red stripes that swept to the floor. The whole concoction magically hinted at sensuality.

What had she been thinking?

She knew the answer to that. In a moment of insanity she had wanted to make absolutely sure that Marcus had eyes for no other woman than her—had wanted to wear a dress that would dazzle him and court his admiration, would summon that dark appreciation and desire to his eyes.

But now caution blew a cold cloud over the idea. Last time she had dressed to dazzle it had been for Dean. But Marcus wasn't Dean. He might be good-looking—OK, gorgeous—and he might be charismatic, but he wasn't controlling and he had no interest whatsoever in a trophy date. Not a jot. And yet she had chosen this dress in all its tantalising glory.

Now, as she looked at her reflection, regret began to trickle in. Because whilst the dress lived up to all Gabrielle had promised it was *more* than the dress. Her eyes sparkled with luminosity and her whole bearing seemed...different. There was no escaping the fact that her hormones had kidnapped her common sense. But only up to a point. Yes, she wanted appreciation, but it would go no further than that.

As she headed from her room, down in the lift and along the corridor to the lobby, anticipation built and scrambled inside her. When she saw Marcus her breath caught in her throat. Forget gorgeous—he looked stratospherically scrumptious. The tuxedo gave him a devil-may-care aura, and the shower-damp hair, the breadth of his shoulders and most of all the fire of approval that lit his dark eyes made her dizzy.

His gaze raked over her, caused heat to flood her veins.

'You look stunning.'

He took a step closer and her heart hopped,

jumped and skipped. Threw in a somersault for good measure.

'But I knew you would look beautiful in whatever you wore.'

Now her heart cartwheeled, and she didn't know what to say except a whispered, 'Thank you. But really it's the dress…not me.'

Silence fell and she sought to fill it before she threw caution to the wind, grabbed the lapels of his tux, kissed him and dragged him straight upstairs.

No, no, no! Say something. Anything, however idiotic, will do.

'I'm hoping it will give me confidence. I don't usually attend events like this—I tend to interview people one on one—very civilised and arranged in advance, in a situation where the interviewees want to talk about themselves. To be honest I'm not very social, so I'm a bit nervous.'

It wasn't working. He was too close—so close she wanted to lean forward and sniff him, to try and identify the scent that seemed to be sending her hormones into overdrive.

Don't do it!

'You can always talk to me,' he pointed out, and

his smile was so wicked that she suspected he knew damn well exactly what she wanted to do.

She needed to get a grip—of something other than him.

Stepping back, she nodded. 'I plan to. After all, that's what I'm being paid to do.' The reminder was as much to herself as to him. 'We'd better go.'

The brief car journey whizzed by, and as she looked out at the dusky grey skies, inhaled the warm evening breeze tinged with mimosa and orange blossom, sensations were tumultuous within her. Everything seemed heightened—her skin was super-sensitive, her whole being attuned to every sound and scent. But most of all she was aware of Marcus.

Then they arrived, and as she stepped out next to him somehow her nerves were quietened by his sheer presence and the reassurance provided by the effortless strength he exuded.

The building itself was sufficient to catch her attention; the sandstone of the embassy gleamed in the moonlight, the turrets and pillars of a bygone era somehow adding to the fairy tale surrealness of the whole evening.

The inside was no less splendid.

'It's magnificent,' she said. 'A pocket of history.'

Without preamble she fumbled in her clutch bag and pulled out her notebook, scribbling down some key words so she could do the setting justice when she wrote the article. The familiarity of writing was a comfort, a nose-thumb at her hormones.

See—I'm here to work, not to relish in physical allure. Ha!

As she returned the book to her bag she looked up to see a familiar couple heading towards them: Rafael Martinez and Cora Derwent, the evening's hosts. Rafael, as ever, looked brooding, whilst Cora smiled in recognition—a smile that held radiance as her red hair glittered under the light of the chandeliers.

'Marcus. Good to see you.' Rafael held his hand out.

Cora kissed April. 'And April as well. I saw you'd been added to the guest list and thought how lovely it was that the two of you had got together.'

April felt tell-tale heat flush her face. Cora's voice held genuine approval and she knew the words had been meant in all sincerity.

'Actually,' she said, irritated that her voice held too much squeak, 'I'm writing an article on Marcus.'

Cora glanced quickly from April to Marcus and then nodded. 'How exciting! That is even more of a coup—and if you do as good a job as you did with Kaitlin and Daniel's wedding then Marcus is in safe hands. And, talking of weddings, how is the royal one going?'

'A security nightmare, I'd imagine?' Rafael interpolated.

'I've had easier assignments,' Marcus said. 'But, more importantly, both Frederick and Sunita told me to convey their congratulations.'

In that instant April realised the reason for Cora's radiance, the glow that lit her from within. Cora's hand went instinctively to curve over the swell of her belly and Rafael's face broke into a smile so broad and awe-filled that tears prickled at the back of April's eyes.

Instinct and a learnt ability to deal with situations like this came to her rescue. She knew that Cora and Rafael deserved the happiness of parenthood, and she truly did wish them all the joy in the world. But still, this glimpse into that serenity could not help but be a reminder of all she had lost.

It was a loss that she could never come to terms with, even while she had had to accept that life went on. That whilst *her* world had collapsed, everyone else's kept on spinning.

'Congratulations from me as well,' she said, suddenly all too aware of Marcus's intent gaze.

'Thank you. We are beyond ecstatic. If you would like to write a lifestyle article on *us* at any point you're more than welcome. After all, we have a lot to thank you for.'

'You do?' The turn in the conversation was a gift—as long as she could think of Cora as a subject, the current of emotion would be easier to control.

'Yup. Your article on Sunita meant that Frederick found love, and that made Kaitlin very happy.'

'Happy enough to forgive me? I was a thorn in her side when she was with Frederick.'

'You were—but that's because you were after the truth. You knew something wasn't quite right, and now... Now all the Derwents have achieved what we thought to be impossible—a happy-ever-after. And Rafael and I are lucky enough to be having a baby.'

This time April was prepared, and she didn't so much as flinch. Cora glanced round. 'Now, if there's anyone else you have your eye on for an interview I'm happy to introduce you!'

For an insane moment April wanted to refuse, to remain near Marcus. The idea of socialising sent a shiver of anxiety over her skin. During her ill-fated marriage there had been parties aplenty, and she'd grown to loathe them. Dean's critical, watchful gaze had made her clumsy by default, filched all possible enjoyment from the event.

But she wasn't here with Dean, and once, in the dim and distant past before him, April had *loved* parties—had revelled in being in good company, exchanging ideas, dancing, talking, having fun. That April seemed like a stranger now—some-one it was truly impossible for her to believe had been herself. Perhaps tonight she could find an echo of that carefree girl…

Squaring her shoulders, she nodded. 'Thank you, Cora. I'd like that.'

Marcus's gaze lingered on the graceful sway of April's walk, on the natural poise that nonethe-less held a hint of trepidation. How he knew that, he wasn't sure—but he did, and for a moment the urge to follow her nearly overcame his common sense.

'You like her.' Rafael's words were not a question, and Marcus turned to face him.

'She is a writer, on a mission to interview the "real" Marcus Alrikson. You know how I feel about the press.'

'Yet you like her. You should act on it, my friend.'

Marcus shook his head. 'Just because *you* have succumbed to wedded bliss, don't try and pull the rest of us in.'

Rafael smiled. 'Once that is how I felt. Then somehow Cora…she changed my mind and I have no regrets. And now with the baby… I feel truly blessed.'

A twinge of something perilously close to envy pinched a nerve, and Marcus blinked in irritated recognition of the emotion. This was nuts. No way did he want a family—he knew his own limitations and was more than happy to abide by them.

Rafael was shaking his head, almost as if he were questioning his own good fortune. 'Who would have thought it? Not me a couple of years ago—I can tell you that. So, my advice to you? If you like her, at least admit it to *yourself.*'

'It's not a question of liking her or not.' Now he sounded defensive. 'In three days' time she will go her way and I will go mine. End of.'

Rafael raised one dark brow but forbore from comment.

As if to prove his point Marcus made sure to circulate the room—though it took more effort than seemed strictly necessary not to check on April's whereabouts. But he forced himself to succeed, and it was only when a gong was struck to announce dinner that he glimpsed her again as she headed to their table.

Once they were seated, waiters circled with unobtrusive discretion so that it seemed as if wine and food appeared almost magically. A starter that combined baby artichokes with figs and huge tasty almonds was followed by a traditional paella that glistened with saffron-coated rice, embedded with enormous clams and bright red peppers.

Marcus was soon monopolised by a man with decided views on Lycander's overseas policies, but even as he focused on keeping his temper he

felt a sudden tension still April's body, and realised she was no longer a participant in the general hum and chatter of the table.

Fragments of conversation drifted towards him.

'We just can't decide whether to have another
baby or not...'

'How many are you on?'

'Three, but they are all so adorable and they
seem to get better as they grow older.'

'Mind you, I sometimes think teenagers are
more work than toddlers...'

'So amazing to watch them grow into people,
if you know what I mean...'

And then, 'April, I am *so* sorry—you must be
bored stupid. Unless, of course, you have children?'

Her leg clenched next to his, so tightly his own
muscles ached in sympathy, and surely the silence stretched just a little too long before she
answered.

'No, I don't. But, truly, don't stop on account of
me. I'm a lifestyle writer, after all, so it's interesting for me to hear how all of you mix motherhood, your jobs and celebrity.'

The words were casual, and yet instinct

prompted him to lean in. 'I can see a way to combine our conversations. I'd be very interested to hear your views on education…'

And from there the conversation flowed around a plethora of topics, from school reminiscences to weddings.

Throughout, April deflected all attempts to elicit any personal information about her life, whilst garnering plentiful knowledge about others. So by the time the last decadent spoonful of dessert had been scooped up, and Rafael had risen to his feet to make a speech, Marcus knew no more about April than he had before.

Not that it mattered, he reminded himself—after all, her life story was hardly relevant. Instead he focused on Rafael.

'As you know, each year this dinner honours a different charity. This year, with respect and remembrance of Prince Axel, our donation is to Drive for Life. DFL is a charity that pioneers safe driving and helps the victims and survivors of car accidents, including those who are left behind. The parents, children, families and friends of those whose lives have been snatched without notice.'

Although Marcus had known about the chosen charity—a charity he supported wholeheartedly on a personal level—the words touched him with renewed grief as Rafael spoke of those who had suffered through accidents such as the one that had taken Axel.

He wasn't surprised to sense April's reaction—to hear her small intake of breath and feel the tension that stilled her body—Rafael's words were emotive. What he *hadn't* expected was for her to leave… But that was exactly what she did.

A murmured, 'Excuse me,' an additional apology and she was gone.

OK… It could be that she quite simply needed a bathroom break, but that was an unlikely scenario. To leave at this point in Rafael's speech was…if not rude, then close to it. Perhaps the food had disagreed with her and she'd had no choice but to exit.

The minutes ticked on. Rafael sat down to a round of applause and Marcus turned his head towards the door. No sign of her. He could sit here and wonder, or he could follow her.

He headed towards the restrooms as a first port of call and halted outside the Ladies'. Obviously he couldn't go in there, but as he leant back against the wall it soon became clear that no one was handily going to come out and answer his query as to whether April was inside.

So with a quick glance down the corridor he opened the door and entered. Silence. No cry of outrage greeted him, so he called out, 'April?'

Further silence—and then he heard the slightest of shuffles.

Feeling like a first-class idiot, he tried not to think of the ramifications if it *wasn't* April in there... *Lycander's Chief Advisor caught peering under cubicle door in the Ladies'*.

'April? If that is you, please say so now as I'm less than comfortable in here.'

There was a small sigh redolent of tears and his chest squeezed in the sure knowledge she'd been crying. 'Then maybe you shouldn't have followed me. There *is* such a thing as privacy.'

'Are you OK?'

Another silence. Then, 'Not really. I just need five minutes and I'll be back at the table. Please go before we draw attention to our joint absence.'

Marcus hesitated, then realised he really couldn't linger in here, nor force her out. 'OK...'

* * *

April pressed her hands against her eyes. *No more tears...please no, more tears.* But Rafael's speech had plumbed the depths of her soul, forced a replay of her past.

Vivid images had flickered in her brain.

Standing in front of Edward's cot, trying to protect him from Dean's rage. The sound of thunder in the background—a prelude to the storm and the tragedy to come. The dense grey pounding rain and the lash of wind against the windows. The pungent smell of alcohol and hatred that had emanated from her husband. The pain when he'd punched her out of the way and the deadly, deadly fear when he'd snatched Edward up. Her desperate pleas as she'd tried to stop him, reaching up from the floor in supplication...

Somehow she'd dragged herself after him, heard the roar of his sports car as he had gunned it away from the kerb. And then a few hours later the police had been on the doorstep, deluged by the rain...

So in the here and now she'd left the table, knowing she was about to break down, and had made it to the sanctuary of this cubicle, where she had allowed herself to weep silently. She'd swallowed down tears when Marcus had entered and pulled herself together. Now she needed to keep herself together—no more unravelling.

She pushed the cubicle door open and headed to the basin, staring at her reflection in the ornate gilt mirror as she washed her hands and inhaled the scent of rose petals that permeated the air.

It seemed ludicrous now that at the start of the evening she'd almost had a sense of anticipation—had held a small bubble of optimism that it might even be a tad enjoyable. How could it be? Social events invariably brought about conversation that evoked poignant memories—a minefield that she had to prepare herself for. Worse, they prompted the need to dissemble, to erase years of her life, her marriage and her son. Quite simply to pretend her beautiful baby hadn't existed.

Stop. Before Marcus returns to find you.

Somehow the thought of Marcus steadied her, and with one last glance in the gilded mirror she turned and headed for the door. Pulling it open, she screeched to a halt as Marcus pushed himself off the adjacent wall in one lithe movement.

'What on earth are you doing here?'

'Waiting for you.'

'I told you to go back to the table.'

He raised an eyebrow. 'No one told me you were in charge,' he murmured, and the small smile on his lips goose-bumped a little shiver over her skin.

Right now the attraction was a welcome distraction from her grief. For a second she wondered if he somehow knew that.

'So what do you want to do now?' he asked. 'If you like I can drive you back to the hotel.'

For a second temptation beckoned, but she knocked it back. This was a work assignment and she would see it through.

'I appreciate your concern but I am fine. Really. I want to go back in.'

'Then that is what we will do.'

Grateful for his acceptance of her decision, she followed him back down the corridor, re-entering the ballroom as Rafael announced that the dancing would now commence.

'Shall we?' Marcus asked.

For a second she gaped at him. 'Shall we what?'

'Dance?'

Refusal would be the sensible option—she

knew that—yet the simple word *No* refused to materialise on her lips.

'I'm sure your readers will be interested in how I acquit myself on the dance floor.'

He had a point, but deep down she knew that wasn't the true motivation for her desire to dance with him. Right now the pull of attraction was moving her away from the cusp of despair. She wanted to be held in his arms…wanted to be up close and cocooned by his strength and powerful aura.

Dammit. When there was so much heartache in the world, so much tragedy and grief, right here and now it felt important to acknowledge the sheer life-giving force of physical attraction.

'You're right.'

What harm could there be in one dance? Especially when she could kid herself it was for research purposes…

But from the second he placed an arm around her waist and they stepped onto the dance floor research went out of the window. It seemed nonsensical that his touch could burn though the lacy material of her dress, ridiculous that desire should strum her body with a riff causing a fever of combustible proportions.

Her head spun as if she had gone through a portal into a more rarefied atmosphere—a world where she could somehow manage to shut out everything but the here and now. Memories, guilt and despair were all still out there, but they couldn't get into this insulated bubble where all she could be aware of was Marcus.

The beat of his heart under her fingers, the strength of his chest, the feel of his arm around her waist, his clasp light yet firm and somehow full of promise, the smell of him, his proximity...

She looked up at him, fascinated by every molecule of his skin. Instinct dared her to move her hand and brush the nape of his neck. She heard his intake of breath as he pulled her closer—so close she knew he was as aroused as she...

Then memory sheared through her insulation, superimposed an image of the past...ten years before...a college dance...a different time, a different man. A man who had seemed to empower her but in fact had enslaved her, had somehow made her dance to his every tune. *Dean*. She had fallen for him, sucked in by his looks, his charisma, by the arrogance that she had mistaken for confidence. In that dance, that evening, she had believed herself to be on top of the world—whereas in reality she had been on the brink of ruin.

Never again would she let desire shut out all else.

Somehow she managed not to wrest herself from Marcus's grasp. Instead she dropped her hand from his neck to his shoulder and unglued her body from his—there was no other word for it. Shame swathed her. Somehow she focused on a point over his shoulder and tried to suppress the seething sensation inside her.

'April…?'

His voice tested her resolve but didn't break it. All she had to do was conjure up a vision of Dean—not the Dean she'd first danced with, but the man he'd turned out to be and the horrific chain of events that dance had precipitated.

'You OK?'

'Yes. Actually, no.' To her horror, she could hear the anger in her voice, the frustration and the sheer emotion. 'This attraction is wrong. Unless, of course, I'm imagining it?'

Right now she would almost prefer the humiliation of being told it was all one-sided.

'You aren't imagining it and it isn't wrong. It's just unfortunate.'

Unfortunate? Ouch.

Totally perversely, hurt was added to the anger that swirled inside her.

'It's too complicated, given our situation—given that you're researching an article on the "real" Marcus Alrikson.'

April frowned. She got why this attraction sucked from *her* viewpoint, but from his...? Then the penny dropped.

'You think I'll kiss and tell?'

'It's a possibility I have to consider.'

Now her anger upped its ante and turned into rage. Common sense attempted to indicate that he had a point, but she lasered it down. He should know that she would *never* do anything so grubby.

Curbing the urge to really give him something to consider—like a knee straight where it hurt most—she narrowed her eyes. 'I assure you there will be no "tell", because there will be no "kiss".'

He opened his mouth and then closed it again,

and she wondered what he had been going to say. Whatever it was he'd clearly decided against it. Instead he gave a small nod and said, 'That works for me.'

April wasn't sure how she got through the rest of the evening, but spurred on by pure anger she forced herself to circulate, to talk to as many people as possible about their opinion on Marcus Alrikson.

She gritted her teeth as she heard the words 'dedicated,' 'committed', 'drop-dead gorgeous' and 'unapproachable'—that from a woman who had once tried to ask him out. There was also 'ruthless', 'arrogant', 'fair'...

Finally the orchestra played its penultimate dance. Then Cora Derwent took the stage, thanked everyone for their generous donations and announced that there would be one final speech before the last dance—from Marcus Alrikson.

April blinked and sudden guilt touched her. This event had been in memory of Axel. In her own grief she hadn't really thought about how Marcus must be feeling.

He climbed to the podium and stood, at ease, confident that everyone would listen to his words.

'First, don't worry—I'll keep it brief. Second, don't worry—I'm not after any more of the contents of your wallets. I want to take this opportunity to say thank you for your generosity tonight, and I want to say a few words about Prince Axel. And I am not speaking to you now as Chief Advisor to the Prince, but as Axel's best friend.

'Axel was a good man—and I mean that in all senses. He had a sense of honour and he truly cared about Lycander and all its people. He had a vision, and it is a true tragedy that he never had a chance to turn that vision into reality. But that aside, what grieves me most is the knowledge that his life ended way too soon. I grieve because I will never hear his laugh again, never have another beer after a game of squash.

'Axel lost his chance to grow older, to marry and to have children, to feel the Lycandrian sun on his face. For that I grieve. But I promise, Axel, my old friend, that your memory will live on; I miss you as a friend as well as a ruler I would have been proud to serve.' He lifted his glass. 'To Axel.'

April blinked back tears, wishing with a familiar fierceness that somehow she could change her past. Those words echoed her own grief—that Edward would never grow older, play football, attend school...

Applause broke out as everyone in the room lifted their glasses, and then the orchestra started to play the last tune of the night and people began to congregate on the dance floor.

April headed straight to Marcus. 'I'm sorry,' she said.

'For what?'

'For not realising this evening must be hard for you, too. Because of Axel.'

His gaze sharpened, and too late she realised her slip: the addition of the word 'too' had been a tacit admission of her own state.

'Yes, it is. But I know that charities like DFL work hard to prevent similar tragedies. Axel would have approved of that.'

'I get that, but it's still hard.'

'Yes.'

April took a deep breath. 'Can we forget about earlier?'

'Yes. I'm sorry, too. I shouldn't have been so tactless.'

There was a small silence and then April looked up at him. 'Can I ask you something? Off the record?'

'You can *ask*.'

'How do you deal with the grief?'

Marcus hesitated. Then, 'I'll show you.'

CHAPTER SEVEN

As THEY CLIMBED into the chauffeur-driven car Marcus wondered if this was a good idea. Then again, were *any* of his ideas with regard to April good ones? Somehow he thought not. That dance? *Very* bad idea; his body still hadn't got over it. His agreement to her writing an article on 'the real Marcus Alrikson'? Also not one of his better moments.

And now he had chosen to prolong their time together. But he could sense her pain, her grief, and like it or not he wanted to help in some way.

'Alrikson Security, please, Roberto.'

As the vehicle made its smooth way through mostly deserted roads Marcus leant back against the leather seat.

'When Axel died, at first I quite simply didn't believe it. It didn't seem possible that a man I had spoken to mere hours before could be gone. The sheer surrealness of it stunned me. It seemed impossible that I couldn't do something to change fate's decree. That I couldn't turn the clock back.'

Just as he hadn't been able to after the fire—hadn't been able to alter the moment when he hadn't gone back in.

'When I finally accepted he was gone, I raged.'

He had contemplated drowning his grief in a bottle; he'd known from observation that alcohol could numb everything, wipe it all out. But he'd also known that that way lay addiction and misery—his genes might point to that option, but he would never make the choices his parents had made.

'What did you do?'

The car pulled up outside the sleek headquarters of his company and they alighted. Marcus keyed them in and led the way to the lifts, pressing the button for the basement. Minutes later they were in the underground gym he'd had installed.

'I took it out on a punch bag. For hours.' Until sheer exhaustion had temporarily anaesthetised his pain. 'Day after day.' A pause. 'Do you want to try it?'

'Me? Punch a bag? I couldn't.'

'Why not?'

'Because it's… I'd feel stupid. I'm hardly fighting fit—I doubt I'd make much of an impact. I can't remember the last time I went to the gym.'

'It's not a competition or a test. It's a way to unleash all those feelings. The anger, the grief, the rage…'

She shook her head. 'I'd rather not feel them at all.'

'At the end of a workout you'll be too numbed by exhaustion to feel *anything*.'

He could see that the idea appealed. But, 'I couldn't do it anyway. Not in this dress.'

'You can borrow some of my workout clothes. It's up to you. If you don't feel comfortable, don't do it. But don't worry about looking stupid or being weak. You're neither. It's a way to stay in control. You control the feelings; they don't control you.'

April stared at the punch bag and then nodded. 'OK. Thank you. I'd like to give it a try.'

'Changing rooms are this way.'

April looked at the T-shirt and, succumbing to temptation, held it to her face. It smelt freshly laundered—not even the faintest Marcus scent discernible. Yet the idea that this material had once touched his skin added a frisson to the emotional whirlpool that already twisted inside her as she tugged the soft cotton garment over her head.

She closed her eyes. What was *wrong* with her? Had she completely lost the plot?

That was a no-brainer. The plot had been left behind long ago that day—possibly in Gabrielle's boutique. Now she appeared to be winging it without a script.

She tried to picture herself actually aiming a punch, and to her own surprise felt a strange thrill course through her body at the prospect. Because right now she was all over the place and she loathed it. If she really could rid herself of the intensity of these sensations then it was a win-win situation. Because once they were gone she would make damn sure they didn't come back.

The thought propelled her into the oversized shorts. Tugging at the cord, she cinched them round her waist, and a couple of expert rolls of the waistband rendered them acceptable. The movement was a reminder of those carefree school days when she and her friends had hitched their school skirts to madly short lengths the moment they were out of parental sight. Days so long ago, when her life had stretched before her full of glorious possibility.

And then Dean had entered it…

Emotions swirled again, and she left the changing room and headed back to the gym, where she halted on the threshold, frozen into immobility.

Just great!

Marcus, too, had changed—into tracksuit bottoms and a T-shirt that seemed moulded to his upper torso. Honed muscles were on display, and suddenly her mouth was dry and her lungs seemed to have forgotten their function.

'Hey.'

He smiled at her and she forced herself not to close her eyes.

'I thought it would be easier if I show you the best way to do this, as well as explain it. There are some things you need to know before I can let you loose.'

His common-sense tone was exactly what she needed to make this whole situation less surreal, and she listened as he explained, his deep voice

full of reassurance as he reiterated the importance of not tensing up and maintaining balance.

'So now I'll show you...'

April tried to treat it as a lesson, tried to focus
only on the technical aspects, but it quite simply
wasn't possible. Not when the sheer glory of his
sculpted body was on display and his grace, agil-
ity and clean movement as he jabbed the punch
bag caused havoc with her insides.

'You ready?' he asked.

'Yes.'

With an effort she calmed her breathing, tried
to pretend this was all research for an article, but
for once her brain let her down, left her unable
to formulate sentences.

'I'll tape your hands to protect them, and don't
forget—'

'To keep my wrists straight,' she finished.

However hard she tried, she couldn't disguise
the tremble in her fingers as she held out her
hands—couldn't hold back the audible intake
of breath as he wrapped the tape around them.
Every movement felt like a caress.

'OK. You're good to go. Remember—not too
forceful the first time.'

She pulled back and hit the bag, jarred her hand.

'Keep it easy. Imagine getting rid of the anger, the grief, but remember *you're* the one in control—you're in charge.'

The deep timbre of his voice washed over her, calling to something inside her. The punch bag came into sharp focus, and somewhere inside her feelings began to burgeon. Grief rolled out its black carpet alongside anger...rage that life had inflicted such tragedy on her, fury with herself for her own culpable part in it.

The punch bag seemed to swirl with images— images she wanted to destroy, to pound into oblivion. Again and again.

Then suddenly she was being held back, contained. 'Whoa. Time to stop, April.'

The images faded and she blinked the sweat from her eyes, pulling herself back into the present, where Marcus held her in a loose grip.

'Sorry,' she said.

'No need to apologise. I only stopped you because I was worried you were overdoing it. I don't want you to damage your wrists. How are you feeling now?'

He released her and stepped back as she turned to face him, tried to assess how she felt.

'Drained.'

The anger and grief had gone. She knew they'd be back, but for now they had released their hold.

Meeting his gaze, she ventured a small smile. 'Better, I think.'

His lips turned up in answer. 'Good. I think you may be a natural.'

Was it his smile, or his proximity, or the fact that she had just exposed something of herself? Who knew? All she *did* know was that awareness had started to swirl around them.

Realisation dawned that she might have punched out her anger, but her desire hadn't got the message and had clearly manacled itself inside her. And now it burgeoned into the knowledge that all it would take was one step and their bodies would touch. One movement and she could rest her hand on his chest, feel the wall of muscle through the thin material of his T-shirt.

Bad idea.

But she didn't care.

One step—that was all it took.

Marcus's gaze didn't waver from hers, and his

dark eyes burnt with a desire that matched her own. Without a word he reached for her. His hands curved round her waist in a possessive grip that thrilled her as he tugged her even closer. He lowered his head and his lips met hers, their touch so new, so wonderful, it pierced her very soul. At first it was feather-light, and then, as she parted her lips in a small moan, he deepened the kiss and backed her against the wall. April slid her hands under his T-shirt. Her head spun in the sheer soar and swoop of desire.

'April...'

His voice was ragged now, and she stared at him wide-eyed, bereft because his lips had left hers.

'You said earlier that you didn't want this. If you still feel the same way, now is the time to say so.' He hauled in a breath. 'Before stopping this becomes even harder than it is right now.'

The words took a while to permeate the fog of desire and her emotions warred. How did he have the control to stop? Yet she had to appreciate the fact that he had—that he hadn't taken advantage of the situation and was giving her a choice. A choice she didn't know how to make.

'I—'

At that instant the buzz of his phone saved her, and she watched as he tugged the phone from his pocket, glanced at the screen and answered it. He moved away, and she wondered if he had taken the call simply to give them both some space.

April closed her eyes and felt a sudden hit of mortification—she had behaved like some idiot adolescent, had got carried away by lust in a basement gym, for heaven's sake.

He ended the call and headed back to her.

'I'm sorry,' April said. 'That was a mistake.'

'Yes.'

Hurt twanged as he stepped closer.

'If we decide to act on this attraction I want us both to be happy with the idea and understand the parameters— and I'd rather the setting was not here.'

Oh.

Her heart pounded her ribcage as she pondered his words. 'So you don't think it's a mistake in principle?'

'I don't know.' His mouth twisted ruefully. 'What I *do* know is that it's not just going to vanish, and we need to work out a way to deal with it. But not here and now.'

'No.' It occurred to April how late it was. 'Shall I meet you at the office tomorrow morning?'

'Actually, there's been a change of plan. That's what the call was about. Frederick and Sunita are considering possible honeymoon locations and I'm vetting them for security purposes. Tomorrow we'll go and check out one of them.'

Great! A trip to a honeymoon resort—*exactly* what they needed. But maybe it was. After all, there would be plenty of people there—staff, guests, chaperones galore. How hard could it be?

'OK. That sounds good. Where is it?' Somehow her attempt at normal conversation had induced a false sense of calm within her, allowing her to pretend the kiss hadn't happened.

'In the middle of the ocean. Eden Island, to be precise. It's about four hours from Lycander. Apparently the island was originally owned by a Greek tycoon—he built a single dwelling on it for his wife, who was an artist, and she would go there to paint. He died a few years ago and she died recently. The heir is some distant relative who can't decide whether to sell it or turn it into a resort. In the meantime he has offered it to Frederick and Sunita.'

Single dwelling? So much for the hoped-for staff, chaperones and guests.

April gave a sideways glance at the punch bag. Perhaps she should ask Marcus if they could bring it with them.

CHAPTER EIGHT

MARCUS WAITED FOR April to settle herself into the helicopter cockpit, watching as she glanced around with a visible hint of trepidation. She was clearly in strict writer mode: notebook in hand, pencil tucked endearingly behind one ear, looking slightly uncomfortable in a black and white sun dress rather than the inevitable trousers, T-shirt and blazer combo.

Sidetracked, he couldn't help but comment, 'Nice dress. Another one?'

The hint of a blush touched her cheek even as she glared at him. 'Thank you. Courtesy of Sunita. It was hand-delivered to my hotel room this morning. During our interviews we've discussed clothes and my wardrobe—or lack of it—a lot. Her note said that she was pretty sure that I wouldn't have a dress suitable for a tropical island. So…' She gestured downwards. 'Anyway, I didn't expect a helicopter.'

'I promise I'm a fully qualified and experienced pilot.'

'I'm sure you are. It's just that in my head we were going by boat.'

'This is faster. We should get there early afternoon, have a few hours on the island, then be back late evening.'

'I've read that storms are predicted. Though it's hard to imagine that now.' Outside the heat shimmered with a glaring intensity.

Marcus nodded. 'They are—but not for a couple of days.'

Once airborne, as always, Marcus entered a zone of his own—one in which the power of the aircraft and the sheer magic that enabled him to control its flight through the air took over.

To his relief April was the perfect companion, making no effort to attempt any form of conversation, given the noise levels, and seemingly content to look out of the window, headphones in place. Every so often she would scribble down some notes.

Within two hours they approached Eden Island, the aerial view a panoramic vista. Marcus brought the helicopter to land on the helipad, his sense of achievement at a smooth, perfect landing always a boost.

'I really enjoyed that.' April turned to him, and her smile twisted something in his chest. 'You fly beautifully.'

'Thank you.'

'When did you start?'

'As soon as I could afford it. I'd always dreamed of being able to fly.'

The reason was ludicrous—stemming from the one time he'd believed his father to be sharing something genuine with him. For a minute the memory was so real he could visualise it...

He could see the six-year-old boy he had once been...remember that rare occasion when his father had seemed to feel affection towards his son. The tendril of pride and happiness he'd felt that he was at his father's feet.

'Son, right now it's like I'm soaring over peaks and mountains and it feels *so* damned good.'

Then his own voice: 'I wish I could do that. Will you teach me how?'

There had been the raucous sound of his mother's laughter. 'Let him try some.'

But his father had shaken his head. 'You never

know—maybe there'll be a chance for him to fly in a different way.'

That evening had soon dissolved into misery, but still Marcus treasured that memory, had given it significance because it had been one of the only kindnesses his father had ever shown him—not putting his son on the path to addiction at such a tender age.

'Marcus?'

April's voice tugged him back to the present and he blinked, focused on her face, freshly aware of the beauty of her features.

'Sorry. Yes. Flying was a childhood dream, and when I set up Alrikson Security I decided to make it reality. Now you could say it's a bit of a hobby.'

'An expensive hobby!'

'Sure. But one I can afford.'

She nodded in acknowledgement. 'I know. It's common knowledge that you made your first million well before you were twenty-five.' She paused. 'Does it ever bother you?'

'What?'

'That you have so much when others have so little? Kids like Gemma and Blake?' She raised a hand. 'Don't get me wrong—I know you've earned your money fair and square, that you set up Alrikson Security and made it a global success, but you also had the benefit of a privileged upbringing.'

Also common knowledge. He'd been educated at a prestigious school, had hobnobbed with royalty, no less. Her words tapped into his reservoir of guilt, took him back to the questions that had always dominated his life.

If a fire hadn't ended his parents' life, where would he be? If he'd gone back into the flames and rescued them, would he still have achieved success? Or would he be in prison? Would he have learnt to fly only in his mind, with the aid of drugs?

'Yes, it does bother me. But it wouldn't really benefit Gemma and Blake if I handed my entire fortune over to them. What will help them is change—social change, governmental change—but also I want to give them *choice*. Because there is always choice in life—an instant where you make a decision. An opportunity when you can say yes or no.'

'What if you make the wrong choice?'

Her question was quiet, and he sensed it held a wealth of meaning—regret, wistfulness, despair—and somehow he knew that at some time she, too, had made a decision that caused demons to eat away at her soul.

'Then you have to live with it, and live your life to the very best of your ability.' As he had done for Elvira's sake—his need to make his sister's life worthwhile had always ruled his actions.

Her head tipped to one side as she considered the words, and he wondered what thoughts were crossing her mind. Whatever they were, it seemed she had no intention of sharing them.

Instead she pulled out the notebook. 'Any other hobbies?' she asked.

'I don't really have time for much more than boxing and flying. What about you?'

'No.' As if realising the paucity of the syllable she continued, 'I used to play tennis and the guitar.'

'Did you sing?'

'A little.' She made it sound as if it was so far back in a dim and distant past that she couldn't really remember it. 'But I'm meant to be interviewing *you*, remember?'

And he was here to assess this potential honeymoon location's security risk.

With a nod of acknowledgement he unclasped the seatbelts and they clambered out onto the Tarmac helipad. The heat hit him, enveloped him in a sultry blanket, and next to him April caught her breath.

'It's…incredible. It's every stereotypical island paradise rolled into one. It's got the works—white sand, turquoise waves, palm trees and glorious sunshine.'

Marcus nodded, but in reality all he could see as he stared at the swathes of sun-baked sand broken up by clusters of palm trees were the potential security risks. Frederick's plan was to bypass security altogether—which was clearly not viable. There was nothing to prevent any would-be assassin from simply tooling up in a boat. As for the admittedly less dangerous threat of paparazzi—he might as well put up a welcome banner and serve refreshments.

He glanced around, suddenly uneasy… The heat was almost too oppressive—a reminder of the possibility of an impending storm.

'Let's go and check out the house.'

As far as he was concerned there would need to be a minimum of three security officers patrolling the helipad and any place where a boat could dock. Plus they'd have to rig up some extra temporary accommodation.

April looked at him with curiosity. 'You look distinctly grumpy. Surely when you see a place like this it makes you feel appreciative of its sheer tranquillity?'

'Not right now. Right now all I see is a potential security risk and a forthcoming argument with Frederick. He wants no security, and that is not possible.'

'Well, you can hardly blame him for wanting privacy on his honeymoon.'

'Unfortunately privacy and royalty rarely go hand in hand.'

They reached the house—an idyllic beach villa on stilts, with whitewashed stone walls, a thatched roof and vast windows.

They stepped inside and April gazed around. 'Wow!'

She had a point, and he wasn't surprised that she had her notebook out and was scribbling notes at breakneck speed.

Marcus had known what to expect, but even so the interior impressed him. The front door opened onto a spacious lounge area that led out to a covered veranda, where a woven hammock stretched invitingly next to a two-seater wicker swing chair. The furniture was simple, but solid, and it oozed comfort.

The lounge led into a corridor, from where one door led to a well-equipped white-walled kitchen. As he circled the room he noted that there was egress from this room as well as the front door. He checked the locks and sighed at their simplicity, then opened a door to a huge and well-stocked larder before leading the way back to the corridor and through another door.

The bedroom. They both halted. There was little point in trying to avert his gaze from the four-poster bed that dominated the room—it was a glorious, decadent piece of furniture. White lacy gauze hung from the top and sumptuous pillows beckoned. The whole damn thing positively screamed, *Use me, please!*

They both stood as if transfixed, and he felt awkwardness engulf him.

Really, Marcus?

He was thirty years old and embarrassed by a bed simply because he was with a woman.

He needed to get a grip, but it took an immense effort to step into the room, open the wardrobe doors, then exit onto the outside veranda—yet another security headache. And all made worse by the fact that when he went back inside April was actually inspecting the damn bed. As he watched she ran her fingers over the covers, leant forward to inspect the headboard. The black and white dress moulded to her body and desire leapt inside him, clenching his gut even as he reminded himself of the impossibility of acting on it.

She stood up straight, saw him, and jumped backwards from the bed, pulling the pen from behind her ear and starting to scribble once more.

'I'll need to vet those notes.'

'Why?'

'Because if they *do* honeymoon here the last thing I need from a security point of view is a detailed description of the honeymoon location.'

'OK.'

'No argument?'

To his chagrin he realised he *wanted* an argument. *For real, Marcus?* Was he actually looking to pick a fight out of sheer frustration? Because here and now, in this cosy, intimate honeymoon setting, it seemed important to remember that April and he were closer to adversaries than friends, let alone anything more?

'Of course not. I like Frederick and Sunita—I don't want to compromise their security.'

'If you like them so much, how can you contemplate contributing to toppling their life?'

'Because this isn't personal. It's about whether or not the people of Lycander have a right to know the truth about their ruler.'

He shook his head, suddenly sure that it was more than that. 'I think it *is* personal. This is about you and your belief that Frederick should pay for the decision he made, regardless of his motivations for making it.'

'That makes me sound punitive—as if I am setting myself up to be judge and jury.' Her voice shook with pure anger.

'Aren't you?'

Suddenly he was no longer angry; instead was wondering why she felt such a need for the absolute truth.

'And if you are, then perhaps you need to consider the mitigating circumstances. If Brian Sewell's claims are true, all Frederick did was go along with a white lie—originally told by Axel himself—in order to prevent a possible revolt which would have overturned everything Axel believed in and would have been disastrous for Lycander. From a personal viewpoint, Frederick was perfectly happy with the life he had—he didn't want to rule. But now he is doing everything in his power to be a good ruler, to turn his country around. If you choose to make him pay for that, then that is your choice to make. Just be sure you can live with it.'

April stared at him, eyes wide, and he wasn't sure which emotion was uppermost in her mind— anger or perhaps shock. And still desire urged him to kiss her. *Stupid.*

It was time to go. He turned to close the door to the balcony, and paused to glance up at the sky. Late afternoon and nary a cloud—and yet there was an oppressive feel to the heat.

'We need to go.'

Perhaps the storm was more imminent than expected—but even so Lycander was only a four-hour flight away. It wouldn't break before then.

'Fine.'

There was both anger and hurt in the word, but Marcus refused to react. He'd called it as he'd seen it.

They crossed the beach to the helipad and climbed aboard in silence. Marcus carried out the routine checks, forcing himself to be thorough even as his instinct told him to make haste. It was an instinct honed in childhood to alert him to incipient danger—either on the streets, where gang warfare had been rife, or in his home where his parents' actions had been rendered unpredictable by their addictions.

Once en route he relaxed slightly—only to realise that relaxation had been premature. The helicopter suddenly jolted—almost as though it had encountered some form of resistance in the clear, cloud-free sky…almost as though something had hit the rotor blade. Another jolt. And another.

Next to him, April gave a small gasp but otherwise remained still. Marcus weighed the options—there was clearly a problem but he wasn't sure what it was. That meant… 'I'm turning back. When I land, get down as fast as you can safely and run.'

It seemed unlikely that the aircraft would go up in flames, but he was taking no chances.

She nodded, and admiration touched him at her calmness. Then all his focus was on the helicopter, on getting April to safety. And so, within a scant ninety minutes of leaving, they returned to Eden Island.

April scrambled out of the helicopter and headed away from the helipad at a run. Marcus was right behind her. Once a safe distance away, they stopped and turned to look at the aircraft.

'What happened?' she asked breathlessly, her mind scrambling to catch up with events.

'I'm not sure. My gut reaction is that for some reason the helicopter reacted to the atmosphere in some way—something to do with the incoming storm. That, or it's malfunctioning for other reasons. Either way, it's not safe to fly.'

'So what do we do now?'

'We're stuck here until someone can come out to get us—and that's obviously not advisable until the storm has come and gone.'

April looked at him, horror-struck, her lips slightly parted, her green eyes wide. 'So we're… we're stranded here? In a storm?'

Fear touched her along with the deep visceral sadness and pain that storms evoked in her. The association of storm and tragedy was interwoven into her very soul; the sound of thunder a portent of remembered doom that brought her a cascade of memories of the day of Edward's death.

'There must be something you can do!'

'Such as what?'

'Maybe someone could come and get us in a boat?'

Because right now an imminent storm didn't seem possible—the early evening heat was still intense, the sand baking through the soles of her flip-flops, although the dusky sky did hold a faint scent of rain.

'There is no way I am risking getting someone out here just because you and I can't deal with being stuck here together.'

April closed her eyes. Marcus didn't know about her fear of storms, or the reason why, and she wanted to keep it that way. But it wasn't only the idea of a potential storm that bothered her right now. It was also his words of earlier. They had hit a whole plethora of nerves, and even now they fizzed around her neural network, evoking anger and hurt and horrible uncertainty.

Had she lost her objectivity? Was she *really* a writer motivated by her own personal experiences, made bitter and judgemental by her own horrific mistakes? The idea was so uncomfortable she was almost squirming in the sand.

'Right now,' Marcus continued, 'we'd best focus on battening down the hatches in the house before the storm strikes.'

He was right. She was behaving like an idiot when it was time to act like a professional. 'Sorry. You're right. Let's get back to the villa. How long do you think we'll be stranded here? And how bad do you think it will get?'

'It depends on when the storm hits and how badly. Best to be prepared for the worst-case scenario.'

'In that case I'll check food and supplies. Will the power short out, do you think?'

'It's probable, but I think there's a box of candles in the wardrobe in the bedroom.'

'I'll check there first, then sort out food.'

'Good. I'll go and make sure the windows and doors are safe.'

As she headed to the bedroom she kept her eyes resolutely away from the bed; that was one item of furniture she would *not* be using during her enforced sojourn here.

Opening the wardrobe door, she grabbed the box of candles and carried it through to the kitchen. A quick inspection showed a well-stocked freezer and larder, alongside plenty of bottled water. The kitchen boasted a top-of-the-range oven and an all-singing, all-dancing microwave.

Panic began to surface—she was marooned with a man she was insanely attracted to and a storm was about to break. OK… The best thing to do was to keep busy—so what else could she do?

Well, if they were stuck here for more than a night or two without power they would need food…

April considered the options and then set to work, determined to show Marcus that she was a competent, objective, *together* person.

'That smells good.'

She looked up as the kitchen door opened.

'You sound surprised,' April observed.

'I thought you were checking supplies, not cooking them.'

'I figured if the power goes off we won't be able to heat anything up, and whilst I know we can survive on tinned food I thought it would be a good idea to cook up some food we can eat cold. I'm doing marinated chicken wings, and a rice salad, and I'm cooking up some chickpeas and couscous as well. There's also caviar and crackers, and some very exotic-looking tinned fruit.' She paused. 'How is our security?'

'This place is thankfully pretty sturdy. I'm a little worried about the windows, but if it comes to it we can move into the larder—it's contained, and I suspect was made with the idea of a storm shelter in mind. We'll be all right.'

His air of calm authority gave her some much-needed reassurance.

He gestured to the stove. 'Can I help? It really does smell amazing.'

'No. I'm good.' Cooking was providing her with a semblance of normality. Here in the windowless kitchen it was possible to pretend there was no storm out there. 'Though, to be honest, it's a while since I've cooked from scratch, so odds are the food may not be that good.'

A small frown creased his brow and she hurried on.

'Do you cook?' A deft basting of the chicken wings and she popped them in the oven. 'I may as well interview you whilst I have the chance.' *Professionally.* 'In a typical day, what do you eat?'

'Are you sure anyone will be interested in this?'

'Of course they will. It makes you more human.'

'OK. In the mornings I have a cup of coffee at home. I get to work and maybe have a brioche or a pastry at my desk. At lunch, it depends where I am—if I'm in the office I'll make myself a sandwich or a salad; if I'm out I'll grab something on the run. Then in the evening I have to admit it's usually a takeaway or a ready meal or something pretty basic. Pasta or an omelette. I snack in between on fruit and nuts, and every year I make a resolution to learn how to cook.'

As if uncomfortable with sharing even that much information with the public, he leant back with a small shake of the head.

'What about you? Where did you learn to cook like this?'

'My parents both loved cooking and they made it a family thing. Right from when my sisters and I were little we cooked. The kitchen was the hub of the house and we all loved it.'

Memories came of Rosa, Lauren and herself, all giggling at her father's daft jokes while her mother was stirring a sauce, of her parents' amicable bickering over which herb would work best, the well-thumbed recipe books, the scent of garlic sauteing... Happy memories. Memories she'd once wanted to recreate with her own family and now never would.

Stop. Focus.

'What about your parents? Did they like cooking with you and Elvira?'

'Cooking was never their forte.'

His voice was casual enough, but she sensed a reserve, a careful vetting of his words.

'So you didn't bake with your mum or barbecue with your dad or vice versa?'

'Nope.'

April waited, but that appeared to be it.

'So, give me a day in your life. You get up, go to work, come home?'

'Yup. That may sound dull, but because my work is so diverse it really isn't.'

'So you don't get lonely?'

'Nope.'

'And you've never been tempted to share your life with a partner?'

'Nope.'

April narrowed her eyes, checked the chicken and regrouped. It had been a while since she'd interviewed someone who quite simply didn't want to be interviewed. Truth be told she'd *never* interviewed anyone so reluctant. Perhaps she needed a more open-ended approach.

'Hypothetically speaking, what sort of woman would tempt you to change your stance?'

'That woman doesn't exist—in reality or in La-La Land.'

'How about you pretend that your life depends upon it and describe your ideal woman?'

'I can't. I'm not trying to be difficult—'

'Much...' April muttered.

'But I can't describe someone I can't imagine. I like my own company. I don't have a template for an "ideal woman". In truth, I can't imagine living with anyone, sharing my space…' A small shudder rippled through his body. 'I told you—I can barely make it through a dinner date.'

'You must be able to come up with *something*.'

'It's not that easy. *You* try it—do you have an ideal man? A tick list of attributes?'

The question took her by surprise; none of her interviewees had ever showed any interest in *her*. 'This isn't about me.'

'I know that, but you want me to do something that is a lot harder than you make it sound.'

'No. Because I know you are quite capable of coming up with an ideal woman template. Isn't that what you did for Frederick? Before he met Sunita you believed that Lady Kaitlin Derwent was the ideal woman for Frederick, and presumably you believed that they could make a go of marriage.'

Ha! Her turn to wrong-foot him. But not for long.

He smiled in acknowledgement. 'The Prince's relationships are his own concern.'

'But it *is* true, isn't it, that you believed he should make an alliance based on politics, not love?'

'I agreed with the Prince that as ruler of Lycander he should get married, but I didn't dictate his choice of bride. The choice has always been Frederick's to make, as it is he who will be travelling to the altar with her. Though of course in my role as advisor I can offer advice on the political ramifications of his marriage.'

'And Frederick has chosen to marry Sunita, the woman he loves, rather than a princess or an aristocrat or someone with good connections.'

'Yes, he has.'

'If you were Lycander's ruler would you do the same? Marry for love? Or would you marry for duty?'

'Well, seeing as I am not in love, and see little prospect of that, I would take the latter course.'

'You would sacrifice your single life for the sake of duty?'

'Yes. I suppose I would. But I would make an attempt to minimise the sacrifice—I'd marry someone I liked, who hopefully liked me, and I'd make sure we both had our own space—perhaps even separate houses—and—'

'Good to know romance isn't dead.'

'I'm not romantic.'

'What about love? Do you believe in love?'

'Of course. I just don't believe in it for *me*. That doesn't mean I don't wish happiness for other people. Look at Frederick and Sunita. You interviewed Frederick before he was reunited with Sunita.'

'Yes, back then he was…shut down, cold, reserved. And now…'

'Now he is a man transformed by love. For his fiancée and his son. And of course I wish him happiness.'

'Then why don't you want that happiness for yourself?' It didn't make sense.

'Because it wouldn't work for me. My route to happiness is different. In the same way that some people like to play the ukulele and other people wouldn't know which way up to hold one.'

'You're comparing love to playing the ukulele?'

'Why not? There are people who get a huge amount of joy and happiness from the ukulele, or any other musical instrument, and people like me who have the musical ability and innate talent of a non-performing flea.'

'You can't compare the two.' April frowned.

'Musical skill is a talent, but the ability to love is universal.'

'No. Some people find love comes easily to them. For others it is something that, however hard they practice, they simply can't do. That's why there are so many break-ups and the divorce rate is on the up. I'd rather accept my own limitations and be happy with them. Love is not for me.'

'Why not?' She still didn't get it—and wasn't sure she really bought his spiel.

'Because I don't have any innate ability for it. I'm not a romantic person—which is exactly why I am not on the market for a relationship. Never have been, never will be.'

'Never?'

'Nope. Feel free to check out my romantic history. My slate is clean.'

'So in thirty years you've never been in love, never had a relationship, never been out with anyone?'

'Well, it depends if you count Rita Gillam when I was fifteen—I went out with her for about three weeks and then she dumped me because I wasn't "suitable boyfriend material". By which she meant I didn't spend my money on chocolates or roses and I preferred to spend most of my spare time poring over motorbike magazines. Then there was Laura Hollsworth—I think we lasted four weeks before she figured I didn't come up to scratch. If memory serves me right, I wanted to go and see an action film and she wanted to see a girlie weepie. I suggested we toss a coin to decide and that was it—I was toast.

'Since then there has been a similar theme— the general consensus is that I'm not a good long-term bet. And I think that's fair enough. I love my job, I love my life, and I don't have the time or inclination or *anything* to offer a woman except very short term physical gratification. My current arrangements work. Low-maintenance, mutual pleasure, no risk.'

'No family?'

The words came with an effort and she knew they were infused with a bleakness she had not meant to transmit. They were a reminder of all her own one-time hopes and aspirations. Yet it was a question she had to ask—part of the interview process.

'What about kids?' she persisted.

For a moment an image of Edward crowded her brain, and she wondered how Marcus could willingly forgo the joy of having a child.

'I've accepted that isn't my path. I don't want a relationship, and that means I can't have children. It wouldn't be fair on anyone—most importantly the child.'

His voice was matter-of-fact and yet she was convinced there was a strand of wistfulness in it, an elusive something she couldn't put her finger on. *Daft*—she must be imagining it.

The oven beeped, and she definitely didn't imagine the relief on Marcus's face.

'Excellent,' he said as he sprang to his feet. 'I'm looking forward to this.'

'Really—don't get your hopes up too high. I haven't cooked in a while—cordon bleu it *won't* be.'

A faint frown creased his brow again. 'I'll set the table.'

CHAPTER NINE

MARCUS WATCHED AS April busied herself serving the food. She had completely put him through the wringer with her attempts to extract information he'd rather not have divulged. He could see the quote now: *All the real Marcus Alrikson can offer a woman is short-term physical gratification!* Disastrous.

But right now that wasn't what bothered him most; he felt a sense of injustice. Somehow April had gleaned a whole load of information about him, yet managed to vouchsafe absolutely nothing about herself. Article or not, that didn't seem fair.

'So,' he said. 'What about you?'

'What *about* me?'

'I know you said you don't want a family, but what's your take on relationships?'

'I don't *have* a take—because I'm not interested in a relationship of any sort.' She walked over to the table and placed the platter of food in the middle.

'So you don't date at all?'

'Why is that such a surprise to a man who loathes dates?'

'Because I may not date but, as we've ascertained, I do still enter short-term affairs.'

'Well, I don't.' Gesturing at the food, she added, 'Help yourself.'

Without further ado he sampled the chicken and closed his eyes. 'April, this is truly wonderful.'

She cut a sliver of chicken and tasted it, her brow creased as she concentrated. 'Perhaps a bit too much lemon—or maybe I could have cooked it a little less time—'

'Stop.' Marcus realised what else had been bugging him. 'Every time I say something nice about you, you reject the compliment. It's as if you're waiting for the "but". This food is delicious. Period.'

April stared at him for a long moment. 'Maybe I'm modest.'

'Maybe—but it seems to me that you don't actually believe the compliments. You can't see that the food is lovely, that you looked beautiful in that dress last night.'

'I... I...' She paused, looked down at her plate.

'You need to believe in yourself. That's what I tell Gemma and Blake and all those teenagers. They have to believe in themselves and their own unique talents.'

It was one of the most important skills that he wanted to teach those teenagers in Lycander's poverty stricken areas.

'I *do* believe in myself.' Her voice sounded hesitant, but then she frowned, as though annoyed with herself. 'And I believe in my chicken.'

'Good! Because it is delicious.'

'Thank you. And thank you for pointing out that I can be a bit over-critical of myself. It's a bad habit I thought I'd got rid of.'

Genuine self-annoyance was etched on her face and he knew he'd hit a nerve. 'Any reason for it?'

April hesitated, and then shrugged as if there was no harm in sharing the information. 'A super-critical ex. Everything I cooked, Dean would find some fault with it. It was always a bit burnt, or had a pinch too much salt, or I'd underdone the beef or overcooked the steak... It got to the point where I got so nervous I made more mistakes, and then I suppose the criticism became justified… I used to believe my cooking reflected my emotions—the stews became a little more bitter day by day, the chili con carne a little less spicy, the lemons a bit more sour.'

Her attempt at casualness fell flat—instead sadness permeated her voice now, and he wanted to reach out, hold her, tell her that Dean wasn't worth it.

But before he could do anything a loud crash had him on his feet as a curse dropped from his lips.

Hell. He'd taken his eye off the weather, so intent on his conversation with April that in truth he'd almost forgotten the storm outside. Insulated in the windowless room, it had been easy to forget the reason they were there—easy to forget everything except the woman opposite him.

Fool.

'Wait here.'

'No way. I'm coming with you.'

'No.'

'Yes.' Her mouth set in a line of determination. 'I don't need you to play the hero, Marcus.'

'I'm not playing the hero. I'm being sensible. I don't know how much damage has been done out there. One of us needs to check.'

'Fine.'

He opened the kitchen door and slipped out, banging it shut behind him. He moved down the corridor and into the lounge, where he saw the window had cracked from the impact of an up-rooted tree that the gale had slammed against it.

Swiftly Marcus closed the door and returned to the kitchen, where April had already cleared the table, packing the remaining food into containers. Her face was pale and he noticed her knuckles had whitened where she grasped the table-edge.

'What happened? How bad is it?'

'The window in the lounge has cracked, but not completely shattered as yet. The storm is really going for it now. My plan is to barricade the lounge door in the hope that we can contain the damage to that room. But in case the storm breaks through we need to hole up in the larder.'

'I'll help with the barricade.'

'You don't have to. I can handle it. If you'd feel safer in the larder that's—'

'No. I want to help and I'd rather be doing

something constructive—it will stop my imagination from going into an overdrive of scenarios.'

'OK.'

Admiration touched him at her attitude. Her body language showed her fear as they walked towards the lounge—the clench of her hands, the pallor of her face—but her step did not falter. And once in the lounge, after one glance at the expanse of cracked window, where wind and rain now flung themselves at the glass in a grey lashing of force, she set to work.

It was almost as if her reaction wasn't fear of the storm itself *per se*.

Working quickly, they emptied the room of furniture and then piled it up against the door.

'That's the best we can do,' Marcus said. 'Let's grab some cushions and blankets from the bedroom and then get ourselves into the larder. There's enough room for us to sleep in there if need be.'

To his annoyance there was the smallest of tremors in his voice. *Unbelievable, Alrikson.* A storm was raging out there, and he was thinking about his libido!

'Let's go.'

It didn't take long for Marcus to realise that his libido would be difficult to exclude from the party. The larder, whilst it was spacious for storage, was not really designed to accommodate two adults, let alone allow a sizeable chunk of space between them.

It was an aspect of the larder that had clearly occurred to April as well.

'Well, this is cosy,' she said, and then looked aghast both at the words and the utterly false breeziness she'd uttered them with. 'And *safe*. That's the most important thing, isn't it?'

'Yes, it is.'

Her face creased with worry. 'How bad do you think it will be for Lycander?'

'Hard to say. We put up flood walls recently, but the winds and rains will still cause a lot of damage.'

Frustration suddenly flooded him. He should be there. Helping.

'You *can't* be there,' she said. 'However much you want to be.'

Marcus blinked, wondered since when he'd been so easy to read. Since never.

'I know that. Nonetheless, I could make a difference back there.'

'You've made a difference here. If you hadn't turned the helicopter back we could have died. We could have been caught in this—could have crashed into the sea, could have been blown away... That was your call and you made it. So, yes, we *are* stuck here. But there are emergency services in Lycander. And I'll bet you and Prince Frederick have overhauled them. I bet you've put procedures in place to deal with this. And those procedures will save lives. That is the most important thing—*life*. Anything else can be replaced. So right now this larder is the safest place for you to be.'

Her voice grew serious.

'All we can do is hunker down and hope the storm doesn't get in. We just need to work out a way to pass the time...'

And there was his libido again. The words that she'd meant in all innocence took on a double meaning and silence spread an awkward blanket over them.

April looked around, as if in search of an activity, a distraction. 'How about a game of I Spy?

That's what my parents always suggested on long car journeys.'

'I've never played it,' Marcus said.

It would never have occurred to his birth parents to play *anything* with their children. And, once adopted, Marcus had done his best to stay out of the way, not to intrude on his new family.

He'd known that Louise and Bill Alrikson had adopted him as an add-on—for Elvira's sake. Elvira had been the child they'd craved; they'd certainly not set out to take on a damaged twelve-year-old. And who could blame them? Certainly not Marcus. It had made perfect sense.

So he'd tried to make himself invisible, so that they and Elvira could get on with forging a bond, being a family.

'Marcus?' April's voice tugged him back to the present.

'I Spy it is,' he said.

April looked around the room, her green eyes skittering over all the items on the shelves. 'I spy with my little eye something beginning with C.'

'Coriander.' Marcus was absolutely sure he was right. Her gaze had rested on the herb section for a few extra seconds.

'Nope.'

'How do I know that you aren't changing your mind? Shouldn't you write it down somewhere?'

A roll of her eyes indicated disbelief. 'For a start, C isn't for "cheat". Second—surely we can trust each other to play a kids' game?'

Humph. 'China…cake mix…coffee…cafetière…'

April kept on shaking her head. Sitting there hugging her knees she looked absurdly youthful, and more than a little gleeful at his continued failure.

'There is nothing else in here that begins with a C. Come on, admit it—you're stringing me along.' He'd known trust was overrated.

'Nope. Do you give up?'

Reluctantly, after a final scan of the shelves, he nodded. 'OK. I give up.'

She gave a small crow of laughter and pointed upwards. 'Ceiling.'

'I cannot *believe* I didn't get that.'

'Hey, it's your first game—cut yourself some slack! My turn again.'

Many games later, Marcus shook his head. 'You are clearly an expert in this. You must have gone on a *lot* of car journeys in your childhood.'

'A fair few—and my sisters and I were all fiercely competitive so I had to be good! Especially as I'm the youngest.'

'It sounds like you were close when you were young.'

'We were. I was lucky to have such a lovely childhood—and my parents are still as in love now as they were then. They gave us the right balance of love and care and boundaries. There was lots of laughter and fun, but we were also encouraged to do well and reach our potential.'

'And you're still close now?'

'Yes. We are.'

'So surely you must want to recreate that kind of family life yourself? Yet you told me that you want your life to remain exactly as it is. And if your parents encouraged you to reach your potential, surely you want to advance your career? Move on to more serious journalism…?'

There was so much about April that he didn't understand, and he wanted to.

'It doesn't work like that. My upbringing was fantastic, but that doesn't mean I can magically recreate it. It's not like copying a painting. My life is fine as it is.'

'So this is what you want? To be a celebrity lifestyle writer? To be single? That's all you want for the rest of your days?'

'Yes. Why is that so hard to believe? Don't *you* want to remain single for the rest of your days?'

'Yes, but I haven't signed up to a life of celibacy. And I have goals. I want to learn how to fly a plane and do stunt flying. I want to build more community centres. I want to help take Lycander into the future. Expand my security business.' He shrugged. 'It's important to have dreams.'

April closed her eyes for a moment and then opened them again. 'I appreciate the concern, but why does it matter to you so much?'

'Because you only get one life—and, like you said earlier, that is the most important thing. *Life.* So don't waste the one you have. Make the choice to go for what you want.'

'I *have* made that choice.' Her words held finality. 'My life is how I want it to be.'

As he opened his mouth to argue the overhead light went out, plunging them into darkness, and she gasped. On instinct he reached out and found her hand, clasped it firmly in his.

'I'm OK,' she said. 'It just gave me a shock.

Reminded me of what's going on out there and the havoc a storm can wreak.'

They both waited in silence, straining their ears to see if they could hear the noise of the storm.

'Loss of power isn't unusual,' he said.

'I know. It sounds mad, but I almost forgot the storm is out there. Now…now I can almost hear the howl of the gale.' She took in a deep breath and shifted slightly closer to him in the darkness. 'Sorry. I just hate storms. *Hate* the destruction and tragedy that is going on out there.'

He could hear the raw emotion in her voice and knew that for reasons he wasn't sure of April was hurting. He wanted to offer comfort.

'I know, but we can't control events out there. We have done all we can do, and I don't believe the storm will get in. My earlier checks indicated that the roof has been constructed with storm proofing in mind. Also, the fact the lounge window didn't break is a positive. But, worst-case scenario, if the house starts to break up we stick close together. Protect ourselves with mattresses, rugs and blankets, take cover under the table or the bench. OK?'

Maintaining his grasp on her hand, he reached for the torch with his other and clicked it on.

'We need to conserve the batteries, but let's find the candles now and then maybe you can teach me a few more games to while away the time. I'm sure I spotted a pack of cards somewhere.'

'OK. I'll get the candles. If I'm going to die, I'm damned if I'll die in the dark.'

'You are *not* going to die. Not on my watch.'

'You can't promise that, Marcus.' Her voice was fierce and without compromise. 'I know you will do everything in your power to keep us safe, but you don't have power over life and death.'

Releasing his hand, she rose to her feet, pulled out a couple of candles and positioned them carefully on the floor. Once they were lit he switched the torch off and they both gazed at the flickering flames as a light vanilla and rose petal scent tinged the air.

'You're right,' he said quietly. 'I don't. But I will do my damnedest to keep you safe.'

Never again would he allow anyone to die if he could prevent it.

'I know you will—and of course I hope we

survive,' she said quietly. 'But if we don't, do you have any regrets? Anything you wish you'd done?'

'I have plenty of regrets, but there is nothing I can do about any of them.'

There was no hope of redemption when it came to the fire and its aftermath. Yet a sudden image of his adoptive parents came to his mind. Louise and Bill—he'd never once called them Mum and Dad. They had wanted him to but he hadn't been able to. To have done so would have meant forgetting his birth parents, and he hadn't been able to do that—had felt he owed them some allegiance after all.

Yet Louise and Bill had been there for him—perhaps not as April's parents had, but as much as he'd let them.

'Except... I do wish I'd thanked my parents for everything they did for me.' When they got back to Lycander he would do that. Not with money, but with words. 'What about you? Any regrets?'

'Yes. But the actions and choices I regret are unchangeable.'

For a while there was silence, broken only by the sputter of the candles, and then she turned to him, her face set, her green eyes glittering with intensity.

'There is one regret I would have if I were to die.'

The softness of her voice fluttered over his skin. 'What's that?'

'You.' Her gaze didn't waver. 'In all the years since Dean I haven't felt even a spark of attraction for any man. Until you. So if this is my last night on this earth then I want to act on the attraction.'

His breath caught in his throat, the direct honesty of her statement catching him on the raw, and every fibre of his being wanted to enfold her in his arms. But he didn't.

'And what if this *isn't* your last night on earth?'

'Then...' She shifted closer to him. 'So be it. I will have no regrets in the morning. I *want* this, Marcus. I want *you*. On your terms. What did you say you could offer? Short-term physical gratification? That sounds good to me.'

'Are you sure?'

'Yes.' Leaning forward, she oh-so-gently ran her fingers over the crease in his brow. 'I *am* sure. I want exactly what you described. Something purely physical and at the end we walk away. I don't want to die, whether it is now or in fifty years, wishing I'd taken this opportunity to…to *feel* something. All bases are covered, I promise. No regrets.'

'No regrets,' he echoed as he finally allowed his desire out from under the iron control he'd exerted for so long now.

He turned and pulled her into his arms, the relief so intense he almost ached with it. A tremor shuddered through her body, and at the realisation that her need matched his own all words fled his brain.

Instinct took over, and their movements were made clumsy by urgency as together they pulled at the cushions and blankets, making a makeshift bed on the stone floor.

For a fleeting second he considered the irony of that decadent four-poster bed.

As if she could read his mind, April shook her head. 'It doesn't matter. All that matters is *this*.'

She stood on tiptoe and pressed her lips against his and he realised she was right. Nothing mattered except the sensual sweetness of her lips, her touch on the nape of his neck, the silken strands of her hair under his fingers, the press of her body against his. All that mattered was April.

She gave a small moan as he deepened the kiss, and her fingers slid under his T-shirt and over his chest. His groan mingled with hers and he gently tumbled her down onto the makeshift bed.

And then all was lost.

The danger of the storm was forgotten, though their awareness of the fragility of life burned with an intensity that somehow meshed with desire and strengthened their visceral, primitive need to meld together, to give and receive pleasure...

CHAPTER TEN

APRIL AWOKE AND tried to remember where the hell she was as she inhaled the lingering aroma of vanilla mixed with the scent of cold stone and herbs and spices. The events of the previous day...the previous night—who knew?—flooded back, and for a moment she wondered if they had been a dream. No! It had all been real: the passion, the shared soft laughter and the swoop and soar of joy.

But now...now it was over.

No regrets, she reminded herself. Those hours in his arms couldn't be rued—or repeated.

Opening her eyes, she realised it had been Marcus who had awoken her. Marcus who was standing up, already dressed in jeans. She felt heat tinge her face at the sheer glory of his body. He smiled down at her, a genuine upturn of his lips, but it held a hint of wariness matched by the expression in his dark blue eyes.

'Morning,' he said.

'Good morning.' *Deep breath.* 'What now?'

For a second she hoped he would lie down again, so that they could resume where they'd left off. But that wasn't the agreement and, more to the point…

'Do you think the storm is over?'

'I'm hoping so. I haven't heard any sounds in the past few hours to indicate that it made its way in, but either way I think it's time to check.'

It occurred to her that he hadn't slept; she felt incredulity that *she* had. But she had. Exhausted, sated, and most embarrassingly *safe*, she'd fallen asleep in his arms.

'Good plan. I'll get ready.'

By which she meant somehow transform herself from fully unclothed to fully dressed. Given the fact that the storm might have caused untold havoc, and given what they had done just hours before, April knew it was ridiculous to feel a sense of awkwardness. But, like it or not, she did.

As if he sensed the problem, he gathered up her clothes without comment or any trace of discomfort and handed them to her, then turned away as she wriggled around under the blankets. Perversely, his tact twanged a nerve—he could at least cast a furtive look in her direction, try to sneak a final glance. Only Marcus didn't work like that. It was physical satisfaction followed by a walk away without a backward glance.

'Ready?' he asked, as if he couldn't wait to take those first steps.

'Ready.'

As they both reached the door he halted. 'April. About last night...'

She shook her head. 'I told you I agreed to your terms. Hell, I *wanted* your terms. Now it's time for the walking away part. We can't walk away from each other quite yet, but we can walk away from what happened. With no regrets. At all.'

'Good. Let's go and see what's happened.'

Trepidation filled her as he pushed the larder door open and they stepped out. The kitchen was untouched, their barricade still against the door. Swiftly they moved forward, shifted the table and stepped into the corridor.

'Oh.'

April bit her lip at the sight of the chaos— the walls were drenched and the lounge barricades hadn't held up. Debris and splintered wood daubed the floor. The lounge was wrecked—the windows completely shattered, everything a sodden broken mess—and the bedroom had fared little better, though the heavy bed remained intact.

For a second sadness pierced her that the idyllic single dwelling a man had made for the woman he loved had come to this.

Yet as she gazed outside it seemed almost impossible to believe. The blue sky was studded with white clouds and the newly risen sun promised a day of heat and balmy breezes.

'Listen.'

A sound drifted in through the glassless window space: the unmistakable drone of a helicopter.

'Come on.'

April followed Marcus as he strode across the sand towards the helipad, where a craft bearing the royal crown was coming into land.

A pilot waved and soon alighted. 'Are you OK?'

'We're fine. How bad is the damage?'

'Bad. The Prince and Princess-to-be are out with the emergency services, but His Highness ordered me to come out here as soon as it was safe to fly, in case you were in trouble.'

'We're fine, but we need to get back so this is much appreciated. We're ready to go.'

'Um…' April hesitated. 'I know it's important to get back fast, but could we check to see if the food is salvageable? Obviously the food in the freezer will have defrosted, and there is a lot of it. If we took it back we could hand it out…'

Perhaps it was foolish—with Marcus's wealth he could afford to buy the contents of the freezer a hundred times over. But somehow the idea of leaving food to decay in the heat seemed wrong.

Half an hour later they were airborne. April looked down on the island where she'd experienced so much and a jolt of wonder shot through her. So many emotions had come into play—so many sensations she'd thought she'd never feel again. Even now her skin still hummed with the afterglow of pleasure, even as she braced herself for the aftermath of the storm.

Marcus dropped his phone onto the seat beside him. 'The community centre got hit—it stood up to the storm, but…'

April felt her blood run cold. 'Was anyone hurt?'

'Yes. Mia and Charlie. Gemma and Blake res-

cued them; they realised they hadn't been evac-
uated and went back in. The kitchen wasn't
properly secured; a window had been left open
and the gale had shot in and swept things off the
shelves. Mia got hit and was knocked out, and
Charlie, left to his own devices, crawled off.'

Rubbing her hands up and down her arms, April
shivered despite the glare of the sun through the
chopper windows. 'Are they all right?'

'Yes. Still in hospital for observation, but there
is no cause for concern—thanks to Gemma and
Blake.'

'That was brave of them—to go back in.'

'Yes, it was.'

April frowned—there was pride in his tone
and in his stance, but there was something else
as well. Pain and bleakness and a flash of self-
loathing. Which didn't make sense unless…

'If you had been there *you* would have gone in,
but you couldn't be there.'

'I know.'

April frowned. He clearly wasn't beating himself up over his absence. So what *was* he beating
himself up for?

A few phone calls later he said, 'We'll go to the

community centre first, then visit the hospital, and then we'll go wherever we're most needed.'

'It's a plan.'

A good plan, that would keep them busy. Already Eden Island had begun to take on a dreamlike quality against the backdrop of how the storm had affected Lycander.

Once they'd arrived at the centre Marcus strode from the chauffeured car and then slowed. For a moment they watched, unobserved.

The building gave off an aura of business and purpose. Groups of teens were busy at restoration tasks, someone had set up some music, and it seemed clear that the community had come together to restore the centre.

'Marcus!' A teen dressed in overalls headed at speed towards him, her blonde ponytail swinging. She launched herself against his chest and hugged him. 'We were worried about you. When you didn't turn up here we thought...'

'I'm fine, Gemma. Are *you* all right? I heard what you and Blake did—you are both incredible.'

'Thank you. We figured it's what you would have done.'

April saw his quickly camouflaged wince, but Gemma continued blithely on.

'If you'd been here. Where *were* you?'

'Stranded on an island,' he explained. 'But right now it looks like there's work to do.'

Gemma nodded. 'Blake and I and some of the others have set up the centre as a makeshift shelter for those whose homes have been destroyed, but obviously we have to make sure it's safe. We're also really missing Mia in the kitchen, because people need food. So many of the buildings here didn't stand up to the storm—there are lots of people who have lost everything.'

Marcus nodded. 'You're doing a fabulous job, Gemma.'

'Thank you. But I'm glad you're here.'

'Thanks to April we have some provisions with us, and—'

'If you like I can take over kitchen duty until Mia gets back.'

The words had come out before April had even realised she would utter them. For a second she wanted to call them back, her instincts telling her not to get involved. She *observed* life—she didn't participate.

Yet Marcus's words echoed in her brain. *'You have to live your life to the best of your ability.'*

'Really?' Gemma's face lit up. 'Can you cook?'

'Yes. I can. I'm happy to try and sort out the food donations and then work out what we need and ways to pass excess stuff on before it goes out of date. I'll talk to Mia as well. If you could give me some helpers, I'll get the food we do have stored safely and get started.'

'And I'll organise an official safety check,' Marcus said.

April nodded and headed towards the kitchen, rolled up her sleeves and got stuck in, directing the four youths allocated to her by Gemma.

It was a good couple of hours before Marcus entered the kitchen, his face dirt-streaked, his dark hair unkempt—he looked utterly gorgeous and her idiotic heart did a funny little leap.

'If you're ready, we could go to the hospital now?'

'Perfect. Thank you, everyone. I'll be back tomorrow at about six a.m.'

There was some good-natured moaning, but all four teenagers promised to turn up to help.

Once in the car, Marcus glanced sideways at her. 'This is good of you, but it's nothing to do with your actual job. How will you manage the time?'

'Kathy will understand that my deadlines need to be flexible.' In truth, oddly enough, she didn't care if her editor *didn't* understand. 'I can rearrange anything in my diary. This is more important.'

Five years before a storm had played its part in the wreckage of her life. Without the torrential rain it was possible that, despite his intoxicated state, Dean wouldn't have crashed the car. Now she was in a position to help, in however small a way. Help others whose lives had been devastated. She wanted to do that.

'It's the least I can do. Some of those teens have lost so much, and yet they are still thinking about others. How bad is it elsewhere?'

'I've spoken with Frederick. He's in the lower district, helping the emergency services evacuate a building with about twenty trapped in it. And Sunita's set up a nursery/childcare centre at the palace.'

The car soon pulled up at the hospital, and they entered the slightly dilapidated building. But April noted that whilst the décor might lack style it was scrupulously clean, and the staff had an energised, competent air that signalled reassurance.

A nurse directed them to Mia's ward and ushered them to her bed. She was sitting up, with Charlie next to her, and April's step faltered, despite the fact that she should have been prepared for this.

'Marcus.' Mia's face lit up, and so too did her son's.

Charlie scrambled across the bed and Marcus stepped forward to scoop him up. 'Hey, little fella. I hear you've had a bit of an adventure since I saw you last.'

Charlie beamed and promptly grabbed a chunk of Marcus's hair.

'How are you, Mia?'

'I am fine, and more importantly so is Charlie—thanks to Gemma and Blake. I don't know how to thank them.'

April pulled herself together, took a seat by the bed and soon engaged Mia in conversation about the kitchen and how she could best help.

But all the while she was oh-so-aware of Marcus as he sat on the floor with Charlie. Her heart twisted as she watched them, and sheer relief that Charlie had survived collided with her grief that

Edward hadn't. Both events had been brought about by what seemed like chance—a collision of the planets, a string of circumstances that had resulted in joy and tragedy respectively. A child had lived and a child had died.

A child.

As she gazed at Charlie, so reminding her of Edward, somewhere in the deep recesses of her brain a warning bell began to toll.

Last night they hadn't used anything...

She pushed the thought away, unable even to contemplate its enormity. Panic circulated in her veins like some deadly virus, and she forced her vocal cords to work, needing spoken words to drown out the reality that buzzed in her brain.

'So there are more provisions in the cellar?' she asked.

Mia cast her a curious look. 'Yes, but I want to tell you about the oven—it is a little temperamental, but all you have to remember is...'

Focus.

But without thought April moved her hand to touch her tummy. Too late, she saw that Marcus was watching her, his dark eyes thoughtful, and she snatched her hand away.

CHAPTER ELEVEN

ONE SIMPLE GESTURE and the world had crashed around his head. How could he have been so *stupid*? Why had protection not so much as occurred to him?

Frantically he cast his mind back.

'I don't want to die, whether it is now or in fifty years, wishing I'd taken this opportunity to...to feel something. All bases are covered, I promise. No regrets.'

Had he been fool enough to take 'all bases are covered'—that ambiguous phrase—as an assertion that she had contraception covered? Why had he not asked...considered...*thought*? He had no answer—not a one—because back then, cocooned from the storm, all that had mattered was the moment.

Worse than an adolescent.

Panic waved tumultuously in his gut as he tried to assimilate the possibility that April might be pregnant.

Chill out.

There was a chance that he had completely misinterpreted her gesture. He looked at April, noted the pallor of her skin, the twist of her hands in her lap.

Charlie gave a gurgle of protest and Marcus realised he had allowed himself to be distracted from the tower-building game they were involved in. Carefully he balanced the final brick, and with a huge beam Charlie swatted the tower over.

'Craaaaaaash!' Marcus said, and was rewarded by another smile.

Before they could embark on a repeat performance, an older woman entered the room. 'Hi, Mama,' Mia said from the bed.

'Hi, sweetheart.' The woman looked tired, but her smile was full of love. 'Sorry I took so long. I needed to give Mrs Martini a hand back from the shops.'

'No problem. Charlie is having a whale of a time.'

Marcus rose to his feet, scooping Charlie up with him. 'Good to see you again, Mrs Hernandez.'

'And you.' She took her grandson, who tumbled happily into her arms.

'This is April,' Mia said. 'She's going to help out at the centre until I'm better.'

Marcus watched as April came forward and engaged in polite conversation, studying her every feature, the silhouette of her slender body, and he wondered…wondered…wondered.

There was only one way to find out.

Stepping towards the bed, he smiled down at Mia. 'You take care. I'll be back to visit soon.'

Minutes later they exited the hospital and April nigh on scurried ahead.

'I'll get a taxi back to my hotel and head to the centre first thing in the morning.' A deep breath. 'I think, given the circumstances, we can call it a day now. I have plenty for the article and—'

'Given the circumstances, we need to talk.'

'Really, we don't. Are you worried that I'll write about last night? Of course I won't—that was between us.'

'We need to talk. If you want to have this conversation on the street, here and now, fine. Or we can go back to my place.'

For a moment he thought she would make a run for it, and then she shrugged. 'Fine. We'll go back to your place.'

There was nothing further to say. The idea of small talk—of *any* talk apart from the question that burnt his lips—was impossible.

They climbed into the car and Marcus directed his driver to take them home, ignoring the expression of surprise on Roberto's usually impassive features. After all it was understandable—he had never before taken a woman back to his home, unless you counted Elvira.

As they pulled up outside the luxury penthouse building that he had spent so much money on and so little time in, he realised that it wasn't really a home—it was a place to stay. A place that represented proof of his wealth and status, showed him how far he had come from the slums of outer Lycander. It was a symbol, a bachelor pad—not a place where anyone would have a child.

Whoa. Hold your horses, Alrikson.

It could be that he had this all wrong and had totally misinterpreted that single gesture.

Yet as they entered his uncluttered lounge, with its vast windowed wall that led out onto a rooftop terrace overlooking Lycander, giving a view of the palace's spires and the city's historic landmarks, and he could ask the question, suddenly he no longer wanted to.

Instead… 'What would you like to eat?'

'I'm not hungry.'

'You must be hungry. By my reckoning, neither of us have eaten properly since yesterday. And you need to eat.'

After all she might be eating for two.

The idea wrenched his gut with an emotion he couldn't catch hold of. Fear, panic, and through all that a silver strand of irrational awe.

'Why?' Suspicion curdled her voice.

'Tomorrow will be a full-on day. I'll rustle up something.'

'I thought you couldn't cook.'

'I can't—but I can boil pasta and heat up a sauce.'

As if recognising that he wouldn't take no for an answer, she nodded. 'OK. Thank you.'

He gestured to the enormous glass dining table and watched as she perched on a chair and stared out over the rooftops, her gaze averted from his. 'I won't be long.'

Half an hour later she looked up from her empty plate. 'You were right. I *did* need that.'

Now he knew he could wait no longer. 'Is there a chance that you are pregnant?'

Her hesitation said it all, and was followed by, 'I'm sorry, Marcus. I can't believe I didn't think…didn't…'

He could see her agitation as she twisted her hands together and he pushed his plate away, reached out to cover her hands. His heart-rate had accelerated in sheer reaction, he felt disembodied, giddy…

'You don't need to apologise. I am as much to blame as you. How likely is it that you're pregnant?'

'It's definitely a possibility, but I just don't know. My period isn't always reliable, but I'm due in about a week or so. All I can do is wait.' Extracting her hands, she rose. 'I'll let you know one way or the other, but I expect nothing from you. Last night was my idea and my responsibility.'

'If you are pregnant the baby is *our* responsibility.'

The word *baby* seemed to rock her backwards, her arms wrapped around her midriff. He rose and walked around the table, pulling her resistant body against his, and held her. Despite her rigidity she didn't push him away, so he stroked his hand down her back, uttering soothing noises.

'If you *are* pregnant we'll work it out. You're not alone in this, April.'

Words which had had the intent of reassurance instead caused her to stand back and utter a low cry of, 'No!'

'What do you mean?'

She hauled in a deep breath and dropped her hands to her sides. 'I mean *we* won't be working anything out. If I *am* pregnant any decision about the…the baby…is mine to make. Alone.'

'Absolutely not. If you are pregnant we would have made that baby together. You and me. So any decision is *ours*.' Fear gripped him. 'If you are planning to have a termination then—'

'I'm not!' Her voice broke. 'I'm not going to do that. Not because I don't believe a woman has a right to make exactly that choice, but because that is not what I'd want to do. If I am pregnant then I will not have a termination—you have my word on that.'

Anger obscured his hurt. 'So you are basically

saying that it will be *your* decision whether or not I can be part of the baby's life?'

'Yes, I am.'

This was daft. 'Why don't we save this conversation until a week's time, when we know whether we even need to have it?'

'OK.' Her relief was palpable. 'Good plan. I'll quickly use the bathroom and then call a taxi to take me to the hotel.'

'Roberto can take you.'

'Thank you.'

April stared at her reflection in the bathroom mirror, at the smudges of exhaustion and the green sheen of panic that clouded her eyes. Disbelief at her own stupidity dizzied her.

Oh, God... What was she going to do?

Well, what she was *not* going to do was break down. For a start, she might not be pregnant. But if she was, she knew the way forward—there was no way she could have a baby. The idea sent a surge of terror, anxiety and pain straight through her. No baby deserved a mother who had demonstrated such irresponsibility in her first shot at parenthood.

She had loved Edward with every fibre of her being, and yet her actions had set off a chain reaction that had resulted in his death. The thought of taking on the responsibility of motherhood again was impossible. Yet she had also meant every word she'd said to Marcus; she would not terminate a pregnancy.

Which left only one option.

Steeling herself, she returned to the sleek lounge. 'OK. I'll let you know what the test result is in a week.'

'Whoa. Not so fast. I've been thinking.'

Great. Just what she needed.

'I want you to spend the week with me.'

'That's nuts. Why on earth would I do that?' The very idea was enough to add the fizz of anxiety to her already overwrought nerves.

'Because if you *are* pregnant then I want to be part of the baby's life. According to you, that is your decision to make—so why not stay here and get to know me better? Plus, this is going to be a stressful week of waiting for us both, so it makes sense for us to spend it together. And...' For a second he looked almost embarrassed. 'And if you *are* pregnant then I want to be part of it. I want to keep an eye on you, make sure you eat properly...'

Warmth touched her at the idea of being looked after—a warmth she doused instantly in a cold stream of reality.

'There is really no need.' Steeling herself, she dug her nails into the palms of her hands and forced herself to meet his gaze. 'Because I know exactly what I will do if I am pregnant—my decision is already made. If I am pregnant I will be giving the baby up for adoption.'

There was silence. His face registered shock, disbelief, and worst of all disappointment. In *her*. And that hurt.

'Why?'

'It doesn't matter why.'

It didn't matter that the idea of giving up a baby half killed her. Bottom line: she knew any baby deserved so much more than she could give. She was too empty, too devastated, too guilty. Another baby would be a shadow, a substitute for Edward, and that was wrong. If there was a baby he deserved a family that felt joyful to have him, the way she had felt about Edward.

'It matters to me.'

'I told you—I don't want my life to change. I have a job and a lifestyle that won't fit a baby. I'd rather my baby had a stable, secure family.'

The words sounded hollow—however hard she tried she couldn't infuse them with even a semblance of truth, and she saw the frown descend on his brow.

'Let's say that's the truth. What about *me*? Do you really, *morally*, believe that it is OK to give *my* baby up?'

She closed her eyes. Why couldn't Marcus be the sort of man who didn't care? In fact, indignation touched her. 'You said yourself that you don't want to be a dad.'

His lips tightened. 'No, I didn't. I said that it wouldn't be fair for me to have a child when I have no wish to be in a long-term relationship, when I can't offer a child the stability of a family unit, and when my work hours are so erratic.'

'Exactly. Adoption would offer a child everything that you've just said you can't give. Parents in a long-term relationship who can offer stability and security. Parents who desperately want a child—who aren't merely doing their duty.'

He shook his head. 'It wouldn't feel right for my

own flesh and blood to know I had rejected him or her because I couldn't be bothered to change my lifestyle to accommodate him.'

The words stung—she couldn't hide the flinch—and his frown deepened.

Before he could say anything, she jumped in. 'So you don't agree with adoption?'

'I didn't say that.'

He paused, clearly weighing up the words he would speak, and there was a sudden ironic tilt to his voice she couldn't compute.

'Sometimes adoption is the best option for a child—circumstances in which the natural parents are truly unfit...alcoholics, drug addicts, violent hardened criminals who would have no idea how to keep a baby safe and loved. Then, of *course* adoption is in the child's best interests. But your motivation is different; you would voluntarily be giving up a baby because motherhood doesn't gel with your lifestyle.'

Condemnation hardened his tone.

'That is your choice. But I don't choose it. I want to be part of this baby's life, if it exists, and I will fight for that right if need be. Or you can make it simple: let me have custody.'

For a second April stared at him, dizzy with emotions. But the one that seared her soul was guilt. How could she contemplate this? Could she truly give her baby up? She quelled the doubt in a torrent of facts. True, she was neither an addict nor a violent criminal—but she had already proved herself unfit for motherhood. Any baby she had would grow up in the shadow of his lost brother, would have to live with a mother who had been emptied of joy, who might slide back into the pit of depression. Her baby deserved the best—and that wasn't April. Could it be Marcus?

She shook her head, the sheer enormity of that question too much. 'I can't do that. I don't know you.'

And God knew her judgement of men was hardly top-notch. Her misjudgement of Dean had led to tragedy. She could not allow herself a replay.

'How can I judge your capacity to be a father? I have no right to judge anyone but myself.'

Big mistake.

An arrested look entered his dark eyes and the anger dimmed. 'Is that what you've done? Judged yourself to be unfit?'

'Marcus. My mind is made up. If I am pregnant I am giving the baby up for adoption. I will inform social services or the adoption agency of your wishes and they can make the call.' She took a deep calming breath. 'Now I am leaving. I'll be in touch in a week.'

'No.'

His voice was firm, and yet thoughtful—she could almost hear the whir of the cogs and wheels of his brain.

'My earlier comments stand. You can stay here. Right now I have nothing but your word that you will contact me or keep me in the loop. You say you can't judge me...you say you don't know me. We can at least remedy the latter. Get to know me. The *real* Marcus Alrikson. I'll prove to you that I am good father material.'

'I can't do that.'

The idea made her tummy swirl, caused nausea to threaten. This was all too much; she wanted to sink into a bed somewhere and wake up when it was all over.

'Because what if I get it wrong, like I did before?'

'I don't understand.'

'I am not a good character judge. I've proved that in the past.'

'With the super-critical ex? Dean?'

'Yes. I married him when I was twenty years old and our marriage lasted four years. In those four years he made me feel worthless. He sapped my confidence, made me feel stupid, ugly, clumsy… Name a negative and I felt it. But at the outset I thought he was wonderful—the ideal man, perfect husband and father material.'

Bitterness coated her tongue, painted her words with vinegar, and her voice broke.

'I was wrong. So I will not—*cannot*—trust my judgement on this. Because if I get it wrong again the baby will suffer, and I won't have that.'

'OK. I understand.'

His face was inscrutable but she could sense his struggle to contain anger—though she suspected the anger was directed at Dean.

'I am truly sorry that he put you through that. More sorry than I can say. All I can do is swear to you that I am not like that and ask you to give me a chance. Ask you to stay with me for this week. Until you can take the test. It's going to be a difficult week. Let's face it together.'

218 MAROONED WITH THE MILLIONAIRE

Weariness touched her, along with a desire to cry. Because there was compassion in his eyes, and how could she refuse a man who was merely asking for the chance to prove himself? What right had she to judge that he wasn't a good man? He had done nothing to indicate anything but decency in his love for his country, his compassion for those teenagers...

'OK,' she said softly.

'Thank you. I'll make up the bed in the spare room.'

To her sheer disbelief her hormones—which must have been on vacation for the past twenty-four hours and had not yet caught up with the action—gave a sharp burst of protest. Cue a mental rolling of her eyes and the sudden desire to burst into tears on his broad chest.

Get real April.

'Thank you,' she said.

Marcus sat at his bedroom window and stared out as dawn crept over the city, turning the sky from grey to golden. Sleep had proved elusive, with his whole body preternaturally aware of April only a few doors away.

Stupid that desire still flared for a woman who planned to give up her baby so she could pursue her lifestyle. But desire wasn't the only emotion in the mix—and when he remembered her explanation of her marriage his hands clenched into fists. An urge to comfort her, just hold her, had vied with an urge to find Dean and use him as a punch bag.

Damn it.

It did not add up. Every instinct he owned told him that April was talking through her hat, her shoes and every other accessory. For a start, he didn't get the impression that she loved her lifestyle. Second, he knew with a bone-deep certainty that she would be a wonderful mother—that the best thing for this hypothetical baby would be April.

So why couldn't she see that? There hadn't been even a hint of indecision in the steel of her voice as she'd stated her intent. But her eyes had told a different story—of misery and despair.

It did not add up. Somewhere the equation was flawed. He had every intention of discovering what was going on, and if April were to be pregnant he would do his best to persuade her to keep the baby. Which, a small voice pointed out, would also be very convenient for him. That way he could be part of the baby's life.

Selfish? Maybe.

Realistic? Absolutely.

Best for the baby? He believed so.

If it proved to be necessary in a week's time, that was what he would fight for. But first, of course, there was a week to get through—a week with April in his home, his sanctuary, his space.

A noise caught his attention and he deduced that his house guest was also awake. Moments later he entered the kitchen, where April was opening a cupboard.

'Sorry. I didn't mean to wake you. I wanted some water before I head off to the centre.'

'Hang on. First you need breakfast.'

'I thought you didn't do breakfast?'

'I don't usually have breakfast at home,' he agreed. 'But I don't usually have guests. I'm sure I can rustle up something. Scrambled eggs on toast?'

April shook her head. 'I'd rather avoid scrambled eggs, just in case…' Her voice trailed off. 'Pregnant women are advised to avoid undercooked eggs. So eggs are fine, but they need to be thoroughly cooked.'

'OK. How about an omelette? Or I have some cereal... I'll go shopping at some point today if you make a list.'

'Cereal is fine. And why don't I shop and cook this week? I really don't mind.'

'OK.'

The domesticity of their conversation was surreal—as was assembling two bowls, a selection of cereal, making coffee for two, and eating at the table rather than standing up at the kitchen counter.

'I've been thinking,' April said as she poured milk onto chocolate flavour cereal stars. 'I'd like to meet your family.'

The request caught him on the hop, and without thought his lips opened to voice emphatic refusal. 'No.'

'Why not?'

'Because they don't need to be involved at this stage. I've never taken a woman home to meet my family and I don't want them to get the wrong impression.'

Or the right one, for that matter.

'I understand that—but we could say it's for the article. I did ask you if I could meet them at the outset.'

'And I said no. I don't like the idea of my family being interviewed about me.'

'Well, it isn't about *your* likes or dislikes. If you are serious about applying for sole custody of a baby, then your family are an integral part of the set-up. I need to meet them.'

'I understand that, and if we discover you are pregnant then you can.'

Even if the thought sent a shiver of discomfort down his spine. Not because he thought Louise and Bill would disgrace him, but because he didn't want April to see how much of an outsider he was in his own family. He had no doubt they would welcome a baby—would love a baby—but that wouldn't change the fundamental distance between him and his adoptive parents.

April shook her head. 'I need to meet them *now*—see what they are like now, when they have no stake in being anything other than what they are. At the end of this week if I *am* pregnant I can't stay here—can't meet your family knowing they'll be judging me for my decision. But I want to meet them—want to know that if there is a baby, and if he ends up with you, he has a good family. Grandparents who will support you and love him. I want to meet them.'

There was anguish in her voice now, and his chest banded in sympathy even as he tried to understand why she would make a decision like this.

'OK. I'll set it up.' Marcus pushed his bowl away in an abrupt movement of sheer frustration. 'But I wish you'd tell me why you're doing this, April. I don't get it.'

'You don't have to.' Weariness slumped her shoulders for a moment, and then she rose to her feet. 'Thank you for agreeing. I promise I'll be discreet. Now, I'd better go.'

CHAPTER TWELVE

APRIL GLANCED DOWN at the message on her phone.

Meeting arranged. Dinner tonight at family house.
M

A flutter of nerves touched her but she quelled them; there was no need for her to worry about the impression she made. This was about her having some information in case she was pregnant. With the key words being 'in case'.

Somehow over the course of the day, as she had cooked and scrubbed, sorted out food donations and thrown herself into helping the hundreds of displaced and hungry people who'd come to the centre, her own worries had receded and some perspective had returned. It hadn't helped that careful calculation of her cycle indicated that it was definitely possible that a baby was on the cards, but the sheer business of the day had meant there was no time to dwell on it.

With a final scrub of the counters and a quick check that everything was prepared for the next day, she exited the centre—then turned as she heard her name being called.

'Hi, Gemma. Is everything OK?'

'Yes. I just wanted to say thank you. Everyone has told us how fantastic you've been—with the food, and the way you've really listened to people and helped them.'

'There is no need to thank me. I have been bowled over by how brave all these people are. God knows I wish I could do more.'

'I think you can. That's what I wanted to ask you. If you'd write about it all—about the centre, about all these people... I know the Prince is doing his best, and I know Marcus is too. But if more awareness could be raised maybe we could fundraise more—maybe we could make the world see that even places like Lycander, where the rich and famous hob-nob, have a darker side.'

For a second April's mind buzzed with the idea and she considered taking it on, getting involved... And then cold, hard sanity screeched in and put a stop to such a nonsensical idea. Getting involved was exactly what had pitchforked her into the horrendous entanglement she was in now.

Ever since she had met Marcus something had happened to her. Willy-nilly, she'd taken a step away from the bubble-like, insulated existence she had created. Prompted by the unfurling of unwanted, unbidden feelings and desires, she'd been stupid enough to expose herself—and it needed to stop now. Before, her life had been the way she wanted it and, dammit, one way or another she had to get back into that bubble.

'I'm sorry, Gemma. I'm a celebrity lifestyle writer. I wouldn't be able to do the story the justice it deserves.'

The disappointment on Gemma's face pierced her, but she forced herself to stand by her words. In six days, no matter what, she would leave Lycander—leave all this behind her.

'You could do it if you wanted to,' Gemma said simply. 'You're choosing not to.'

April tried to think of a response, but knew anything she said would sound like an excuse. How could she explain to Gemma that she might be pregnant, that even if she wasn't she had to get away? The world outside her safe, calm bubble was too bright, too overwhelming, too scary.

'I'm sorry,' was the best she could come up with.

'Don't worry about it. And thank you again for all your help at the centre.'

Swivelling on her heel, Gemma turned back towards the community centre and April tamped down the guilt and headed for the sleek black car that had pulled up at the kerb.

Marcus emerged and opened the door for her, then waited as she slid in before climbing in after her.

'Is everything OK?'

'Fine. It went well today. But it's sad to see all those people who have lost so much. I am impressed with how efficient and well organised the services are—and Frederick has promised temporary accommodation to all who need it and he seems to be making good on that promise.'

She glanced at him.

'That can't be easy to get sorted, and I'm guessing that you have spent a large part of your day on it.' He looked tired, with dark smudges under his eyes, and she wondered when he'd last actually slept.

'It's not only that. It's about how to sort out the housing issue. This can't happen again, so that means new houses will have to be constructed properly. And that means continued upheaval and, of course, a need for revenue.' He shook his head. 'Anyway, that isn't your problem.'

'Are you sure you want to see your parents tonight? I didn't mean it had to be instantly.'

'That's fine—at least we won't have to cook. I've said that you have a dairy allergy. That way you can avoid eggs and unpasteurised cheese or milk without having to explain why.'

Warmth touched her that somewhere in his day Marcus had found time to research the foods that pregnant women needed to avoid.

'Thank you.'

'There is something I need to tell you. It's not a big deal, but it may come up. Elvira and I are adopted.'

It was impossible to read his expression. His features were silhouetted against the dusky Lycander evening. Her brain whirred as she processed the information and its meaning, and guilt smote her anew. Her decision to choose adoption if she was pregnant must have resonated with him on such a deep level.

'I… I don't know what to say.'

'There is no need to say anything.' His voice was flat. 'And please don't jump to any conclusions. Adoption was the very best option for Elvira and for me, and I have nothing but gratitude that we were taken in.'

A glance out of the window and he nodded.

'We're here.'

April blinked, realising he had timed this in such a way that she would have no opportunity to ask questions. In truth, her brain was too abuzz for her even to be able to formulate any. Why hadn't Marcus told her?

Hurt touched her but she focused on her surroundings, wanting to imprint them on her mind so that if it came to it one day she would be able to picture her child here.

She followed Marcus across a gravelled courtyard, saw the sprawl of a beautiful terracotta-hued villa lit by an alluring twinkle of artful fairy lights. The door opened and an elegant woman with ash-blonde hair opened the door.

'Marcus. It is so lovely to see you.' She turned to April, a look of wariness and curiosity in her bright blue eyes. 'And you must be April. I'm Louise. I've read so many of your articles; you have a wonderful turn of phrase.'

'Thank you. It's very kind of you to invite me to dinner.'

'Our pleasure. Come in.'

April followed Louise into a spacious living room, aware of the quiet elegance of its furnishings that created a homely, comfortable atmosphere. A dark-haired man stood in front of a mantelpiece—a man who, oddly enough, reminded her of Marcus. Of course now she knew that the resemblance couldn't be hereditary—so what was it? Perhaps it was the man's stance, his posture of confidence and authority. The smile he gave his wife softened his face, and she could see an unspoken communication pass between them.

'Good evening, April. I'm Bill Alrikson. Can I offer you a drink?'

'I'd love a soft drink—I'm working tonight and I have a busy day tomorrow, so I'd best avoid alcohol.'

Too much information, April.

Louise turned in an abrupt movement and April did her best to look as bland as possible, realising she had taken a step closer to Marcus—a move Louise had also clocked.

Relief swathed her as the door opened and Elvira burst in.

'Big Bro!' she exclaimed, and headed straight for Marcus, giving him a hug. Then, 'Mama... Pops.' Two more hugs and then she turned to April, a smile on her face but wariness rather than welcome in her dark blue eyes.

'So,' Louise said, 'I understand you're writing about "the real Marcus Alrikson". How can we help?'

Straight to the chase.

Belatedly it occurred to April that she should have prepared some questions—she could hardly come out with, *Do you think he'd make a good dad?* Or, *What sort of grandparents would you be?*

'Could you maybe tell me a bit about his childhood?'

Further mistake.

She had no idea when Marcus had been adopted—didn't even know whether he and Elvira were from the same birth family or not.

But Louise didn't bat an eyelid. 'Of course. Marcus was a very serious child, and that's why some of my very favourite memories are of when he laughed or even smiled.' She turned to her husband. 'Do you remember the bicycle?'

'Yes.' Bill stepped forward and handed April a mocktail. 'It was a birthday gift. Marcus never asked for anything, but we were sure he'd love a bike. I still remember his face when he saw it. It lit up.' Bill handed Marcus a whisky. 'And then he offered to pay us back for it.'

'Obviously we refused,' Louise interpolated, with a quick glance at her husband. 'And then he took the bike and disappeared for hours. He came back with cuts and bruises but with another smile on his face because he could ride it. It was a two-smile day!'

'Then there was the time he ran away from boarding school,' Bill said.

Louise shook her head. 'Elvira had just started school, and Marcus took it into his head that he needed to be here to make sure she didn't get bullied.'

The image of a teenage Marcus arriving home to protect his little sister was so vivid in April's head that she blinked to clear it.

'Did it work?' she asked, turning to Elvira, who was watching her with suspicion still evident in her gaze. It occurred to April that the protective instinct worked two ways.

'Of course,' Elvira said, throwing a quick affectionate smile at her brother. 'Mum and Dad let him stay at home and take me to and from school—it set me up for years. All my friends thought he was the coolest thing ever. They all hero-worshipped him and everyone wanted to come to my house in case he was there.'

'Then I guess I made the right call,' Marcus said.

'Well, that's what *we* thought,' Louise said. 'Which is why we squared it with your *very* irate head of house.'

'I didn't know you did that.'

Marcus looked surprised, and Louise smiled at him—a smile that April sensed held an undercurrent of sadness.

Then, as if she'd felt April's gaze, Louise stood up. 'If we're ready, let's head in to dinner.'

Dinner was amazing—the food melt-in-the-mouth incredible. Conversation flowed, orchestrated by Louise and Bill. Topics ranged from politics to business to the nitty-gritty of Elvira's university course.

Marcus played his part—and yet there was something April couldn't put her finger on. It was almost as if Marcus was effacing himself from the conversation.

'This is an amazing house,' April said. 'Did you grow up here?'

'No,' Elvira chipped in. 'We grew up in town—it's where I live now. We converted it into a student house when Mum and Dad moved here a couple of years ago. Marcus gave them this house.'

Marcus frowned, and April knew he hadn't wanted his sister to divulge that fact.

'Time for dessert,' Louise said.

'Can I help?' April offered.

'That would be lovely,' the older woman agreed.

Marcus's frown deepened into a scowl.

April couldn't help it—she grinned down at him as they left. 'Don't look so grumpy, Marcus.

I'm sure Louise has nothing but good things to share about you.'

Before he could answer she hotfooted it after Louise into a typical country kitchen where she felt instantly at home. Louise opened the fridge and pulled out the most decadent chocolate cake April had ever seen.

'Vegan—so it's dairy-free,' Louise said.

'Thank you.' A pang of guilt shot through April. 'I am *so* sorry to put you to so much trouble.'

'It's no trouble.'

Louise extracted a bowl of raspberries and closed the fridge door.

'We didn't want to accept the house,' she said suddenly. 'We knew it was Marcus's way of paying us back and we didn't want that. We never wanted him to feel in our debt, but I know he did. In the end we agreed to take it because it meant so much to him that we did. And because he chose a house he knew I'd always loved. Goodness knows how he persuaded the previous owner to sell, or how much he had to pay for it...' She shrugged. 'I guess I wanted you to know that we aren't after his money.'

'I wouldn't have thought that.'

'Good. So, is there anything else you want to ask me? I can tell you exactly how proud we are of Marcus—of his achievements and his sheer courage and grit. He worked so very hard to catch up on his education—didn't give up even when he realised how far behind he was. And the way he was with Elvira…it was heartbreaking. He looked after her with a gentleness and a love I can't describe. He was and is an amazing brother.'

Louise handed April a stack of plates.

April wanted to ask so much more but restrained herself—she knew that Marcus would loathe the idea that they were discussing him, and yet this was her opportunity to discover more about the man she might have made a baby with. The temptation was great but before she could say another word the door opened and Marcus came in. 'Sorry to interrupt—'

'No, you aren't,' Louise said. 'But don't worry, Marcus, I haven't said anything you wouldn't like. And now it's time for dessert.'

Two pieces of cake and a cup of tea later, April thanked Louise and Bill for the meal.

'I'm glad it was all right. I was surprised at how many of my usual dishes include dairy. I'd love it if you could share some dairy-free recipes with me.'

April blinked. Her mind was a complete blank; not a single dairy-free idea could she come up with. Did pasta contain milk?

'Of course. I'll get your email address from Marcus.'

'Thank you.'

But there was a small frown on Louise's face as she turned to Marcus to say goodbye.

'Take care, both of you.'

'We will. Thank you again.'

April felt a ridiculous pang as she walked towards the car; in all probability she would never see Louise and Bill again. For an insane moment, as the car glided through the midnight-blue darkness, an absurd fantasy filled her mind and she drifted between waking and sleep. Her and Marcus…a couple…herself with a baby in her arms… Louise and Bill looking on… In-laws who liked her…believed in her… Marcus with his arm around her as he gazed down at the tiny precious bundle in her arms.

And then the image faded and changed, and instead she saw herself with Edward as he took his first tottering step…fast-forwarded to weeks later and the police on the doorstep, telling her that Edward was dead…gone…at rest for ever.

April sat bolt-upright with a small cry and instantly Marcus scooted across the seat, his warm bulk next to hers.

'April?'

She blinked. 'I'm fine.'

Oddly enough, she was—after all, those half-dreams had shown her that her decision was right. Tragedy had touched her life irrevocably and she would be tainted for ever. Another baby was an impossible mirage.

'I liked your parents.'

His face was slightly averted, and for a moment he said nothing. Then, 'I'm glad. They are good people.'

'They are clearly very proud of you.'

More silence, though she would swear he had puffed out the smallest *'pah'*.

'Why do I get the impression you don't believe that?'

'I don't know.'

Relief vibrated from him as the car pulled to a stop outside his apartment, but her eyes narrowed in determination—he was *not* going to escape that easily. Louise and Bill *were* proud of him.

Once inside the lounge, she resumed. 'You do *know* they are proud of you, right?'

Discomfort etched his features as he thrust his hands into his pockets. 'April, drop this, OK? I know Louise and Bill are pleased I've done well in life.'

'But that's different from knowing they're proud of you—not because you've made lots of money but because you're the person you are.'

'And I owe them a huge debt. One I will do my best to pay back.'

'How? With *money*?'

'How else? They paid for my education, fed me, clothed me, gave me the means to make my wealth.'

'They are your *parents*—they love you; they don't want your money.' She put her hands on her hips. 'Is this the type of parent you plan to be? Will you be keeping track of every penny you spend and expecting it to be paid back with interest?'

'No! Of course not. That's different.'

'How?'

'I was twelve when Elvira and I were adopted. Elvira was only four. Louise and Bill had never planned to adopt an older child—they wanted a little one. They fell for Elvira and decided out of the goodness of their hearts to take me as well. For Elvira's sake. The social workers couldn't believe it—and neither could I. As I told you, they're good people. So, yes, I do owe them a debt.'

For a moment April wondered how it must have felt to that twelve-year-old boy—to have been taken in out of charity rather than love. And then she remembered Louise's expression when she'd described the bond between Marcus and his sister.

'Perhaps they didn't intend to adopt an older child, but that doesn't mean they took you just for Elvira's sake. Maybe they took you for both your sakes. Whatever their motivation, they grew to love you.'

'You don't have to try to make me feel good about this, April. Love doesn't come into it— their charitable action allowed me to be part of

Elvira's life. I didn't expect anything more from them.'

'Didn't expect or *couldn't* accept?' The question fell from her lips without permission from her brain, and his brows pulled together in a glower.

'Meaning…?'

'Meaning that they love you and you seem to be having difficulty accepting that.'

'Spare me, please. You've spent a few hours over a dinner table with them—that does *not* endow you with the ability to judge their emotional state. Eighteen years ago I was a street kid. I was illiterate, foul-mouthed, and my greatest talent was my ability to fight dirty. Really, I was *not* loveable, and no one in their right mind would have taken me in.'

'But you turned yourself around—surely you see how amazing that is?'

Only he didn't—she could see that in the stubborn jut of his jaw, in the darkness of his expression as he looked back into the past and saw something that she couldn't.

Without thought she moved closer to him,

wanting to make him listen to her, force him to acquiesce to what was so obvious to her.

'Marcus…'

'Drop it, April. You got what you wanted. To meet Louise and Bill. There is absolutely no need for your pseudo-psychology.'

April halted in her tracks; the words made her flinch.

'Or if you do feel the need perhaps you should aim the spotlight at yourself. *You* are the one who wants to give up a baby—your own flesh and blood. Maybe you need me to fall in with all this for yourself, so that you can believe all adoption stories have a happy ending.'

For a moment her feet wanted to move backwards, but she forced herself to remain where she was. Because despite the harshness of his words she recognised that he had a right to say them— that they weren't the kind of put-down that Dean had delighted in. They were the barbs of a man in pain himself.

'You are entitled to that opinion,' she said quietly. 'But it isn't pseudo-psychology to recognise genuine love. You can deny it as much as you like, but your parents love you because you deserve to be loved. And, whether you believe me or not, if I am pregnant I will love this baby more than you can imagine.'

He raised his hand as if to reach out for her, and now she did step backwards.

'I'm heading to bed. I'll see you tomorrow.'

CHAPTER THIRTEEN

EVER SINCE THEIR catastrophic conversation following the disastrous dinner April had avoided him. They met briefly over breakfast and dinner, when they uttered inane civilities, but she remained aloof, hidden behind a veneer of politeness and cool indifference—and Marcus couldn't blame her. He'd behaved like the proverbial horse's backside. Worse, he was too much of a coward even to apologise, in case it sparked another catastrophic conversation.

But things couldn't go on like this. The week was very nearly over and April looked exhausted—so he'd decided today would be different.

Marcus looked at the breakfast he had laid out on the table and waited as he heard April's footsteps approach. She pushed the door open and then checked on the threshold, looking from him to the table. Surprise raised her brows.

'What's this?'

'Pancakes,' he said with a touch of pride. 'Admittedly the second batch—the first ones were a disaster. I wasn't sure what you would want with them, so I thought I'd give you a choice. Bacon, maple syrup, lemon juice, sugar, blueberries—and there's chocolate ice cream in the freezer.'

'You've gone to a lot of trouble.'

Her expression was a near comical mix of wariness and innate politeness, and he grinned.

'It's OK. You don't have to be polite. Just sit down and tuck in.'

Another hesitation and then she shrugged. 'OK.'

Half an hour later satisfaction touched him as she polished off pancake number four.

'I'll tidy up, then I need go,' she said.

'Not so fast. There's been a change of plan.'

'What do you mean?'

'Frederick has ordered us to take a day off, and I've decided to obey the royal command.'

'Well, I haven't. They're expecting me at the community centre and...'

Bracing himself, Marcus shook his head. 'Actually, they aren't. Mia is back now, and I've asked Mrs Hernandez to help out today.'

Her green eyes narrowed and her fingers twitched in a clear desire to pick up her empty plate and hurl it at his head.

'Well, I'm going in anyway.'

'Then at least let me tell you what I have planned for the day. First I am going to spend at least ten minutes apologising for my behaviour the other night. Then I want to take you for a day in the Lycander countryside and a picnic lunch. You've worked yourself into the ground in the past week and you deserve a day of rest. If you really can't stand to go with me I could ask Elvira to go with you—or Gloria, or anyone else you want.'

April stared at him for a long moment. 'Let's start with the apology and go from there.'

Reaching out, he covered her hand with his. 'I'm truly sorry, April. I shouldn't have said what I did. I don't understand why you would give a baby up, because I truly believe you would make a wonderful mother. But I need to trust that you have your reasons—not try to make you feel bad about the decision. Because I do totally believe in your love for a baby.'

Tears sheened her green eyes. 'Thank you.' Her fingers tightened around his. 'I owe you an apology as well. I overstepped. Your relationship with Louise and Bill is your business, and you're right. You lived your whole childhood with them; I spent a few hours with them around a dinner table. That doesn't give me the right to judge.'

It didn't, and yet he hadn't been able to forget her words—had wondered if perhaps he had got it all wrong. *Could* Louise and Bill have grown to love him? The idea didn't seem possible—after all, if that were so wouldn't they have told him?

'Also, I realise now that for you the idea of me giving a baby up for adoption must be even more complicated than it would be for anyone else, and I am truly sorry for that.'

Marcus shook his head; he couldn't let her beat herself up any further. 'I appreciate that—and, yes. of course my circumstances play a part in my reaction. But I *do* believe in adoption in the right circumstances. In our case our birth parents died and we were very lucky to be taken in by Louise and Bill.'

'Marcus, I am so sorry. It must have been devastating to lose your parents. I thought—' She broke off, looking confused.

'You thought I'd been taken away from my birth parents?'

It was fair enough—after all, he'd told her that he'd been an illiterate, foul-mouthed, unloveable street fighter at the time of his adoption.

'I wasn't—though maybe I should have been.' It was another question he tussled with. 'My birth parents were alcoholics, drug addicts, criminals. But—'

'But they were still the only parents you had?'

'Yes.' And as such of course he'd loved them. For all the good it had done him.

With the benefit of hindsight, he understood that the path of addiction his parents had ended up on had distorted their ability to feel, to parent, to love. Their need for the next drink, the next hit, had outweighed anything else. But he also knew they had felt *something* for him, however insubstantial.

'It was complex,' he agreed now, as he pushed thoughts of the past away. He wanted today to be a happy day—to create *good* memories. 'But we've been sidetracked. I don't want today to be about the past, or the future. Let's live in the moment.'

She hesitated, her green eyes wide as they rested on his face, and then she nodded, smiled a smile that lit her face. 'It's a plan.'

'So...a picnic in the countryside?'

'I think that sounds lovely. I'll change into something more suitable for a picnic and then let's go.'

Twenty minutes later she re-entered the kitchen, a tentative smile on her lips and a sliver of doubt in her eyes.

'What do you think?' she asked. 'I literally grabbed it off a clothes stall a couple of days ago, because I knew I was running low on clean clothes and might not have time to do a wash.'

'I think it's beautiful. I think *you're* beautiful.'

The words were out before he could stop them—because they were true. The simple sun dress, a swirl of turquoise and sea-green, accentuated her slender curves and the length of her legs. But it was more than that; her features were relaxed, and her green eyes sparkled with a luminosity they had lacked for the past days.

'Thank you.' She smiled suddenly. 'And please

note my gracious acceptance of the compliment. Now, shall I rustle up a picnic?'

'No need. I've done it. Well, I went to the supermarket and bought some stuff.'

To his considerable relief the very kind lady behind the deli counter had taken pity on him and put together a selection she had promised him would be perfect for a countryside picnic.

'Let's go. I've given Roberto the day off, so it's just you and me.'

Just you and me.

The words seemed to echo in the air, reverberating with promise and anticipation, and Marcus threw caution to the wind and reached out for her hand. Hands clasped, they headed for the car.

As he drove along he could sense April relax as she absorbed the beauty of the Lycandrian countryside—the variety and shades of green hedgerows and leaves, the golden fields and the sun-kissed breeze tinged with the scent of lemons.

'It's so peaceful,' she said. 'It's almost impossible to believe that we're only hours away from the city. Where are we going?'

'A meadow with a river running through it and

a weeping willow where we can sit in the shade and have our picnic. And I've brought a kite.' For a moment he felt like an absolute idiot, and glanced sideways at her to see if she was laughing at him.

But her face was illuminated with a smile that made him catch his breath.

'That sounds idyllic. I haven't flown a kite in years.'

'Neither have I. Louise and Bill brought Elvira here to teach her how and she asked me to come too, so I did.'

For a moment he revisited the memory, and it occurred to him that that wasn't exactly how it had happened. First Bill and Louise had asked *him* and he'd refused—sure that he would be in the way, that he had been asked out of duty. He frowned as he wondered if perhaps…just perhaps… April had a point.

'We're here.'

They alighted from the car and he led the way across the fields to the meadow, and somehow once again it seemed the most natural thing in the world to take her hand. They reached the weeping willow and spread the blanket out under the sweep of its branches, then unpacked an array of delicacies from the wicker basket.

'This is amazing. Thank you.' She bit into a parmesan and gruyere cheese straw and rested back against the tree trunk with a contented sigh. 'One day we should hire a mini-bus and bring the teens out here. Gemma and Blake and Mia… everyone.'

'We will. Lord knows they deserve some peace and quiet…a break.'

'It will be a long time before life goes back to normal for them and their families, won't it?' Her voice sounded sad.

'Yes. But I promise you that the new "normal" will be a lot better than the old one. Frederick and I have been in consultation with city planners and architects, surveyors and construction firms, and it's all coming together. Safe, proper housing is a priority.'

'I know you will make it happen. And that brings me to something I want to tell you. I've decided to drop the story about Axel and Frederick and the night of the tragedy.'

Relief caused him to smile, even as curiosity prompted him to ask, 'Why?'

'Because if there is one thing I've learnt from this tragedy it's that Frederick cares about Lycander and every one of his people, and for me to start a sequence of events that might topple him at a time when Lycander needs him would be wrong.'

'What about the truth?'

'I still believe in the truth, and I still believe that the people deserve that truth. I spoke with Frederick.'

'You did?'

'Yes. Briefly. I told him that I knew but I wouldn't pursue it—and he promised me that one day he will tell the truth, when the time is right. When he's had a chance to prove to everyone that he is not the Playboy Prince they once despised. If Frederick did wrong, he's doing his best to do right now. That's what you told me once, isn't it? That if you have done wrong then sometimes all you can do is live as good a life as you can to redeem yourself. So I'll drop the story.'

'I'm glad,' he said simply.

'There is also the fact that Brian Sewell is scum. I caught him at the community centre the other day, trying to convince everyone that their poor-quality housing was Frederick's fault and they should take to the streets in protest instead of setting up shelters!'

'What happened?'

'I gave him a piece of my mind and Blake and Isaac threw him out. Clearly all that boxing training paid off; he went like a lamb.'

The sheer indignation in her voice showed. 'You really care, don't you?' he said.

The words caused her to pause, an arrested look in her green eyes.

'Why don't you stay?'

'Stay?'

'Yes. In Lycander. For a while. You can base yourself anywhere as a writer, and you could stay on at the centre for a while if you wanted. I know how much help you are there. Perhaps you could even write a piece on the centre...'

His voice trailed off as he wondered what exactly he was asking.

Clearly she was wondering the same. 'Would you want me to stay regardless of whether or not I'm pregnant?'

Yes. The word exploded in his mind and he shook his head. Of course he didn't want April to stay. Obviously he wouldn't mind, because it would make no difference to him. *Could* make no difference to him.

'That would be up to you,' he said evenly. 'But maybe we should wait and see what the test says before we decide anything.' He rose to his feet. 'Now, let's fly that kite.'

As he unpacked the multi-coloured kite he was tantalisingly aware of her proximity: the light scent of orange blossom, the soft silk of her auburn hair so close as they bent over the kite.

'Would you like to go first?'

'Absolutely.'

Soon they were racing across the meadow, both of them whooping with joy as after a few false starts the breeze caught the kite and it swooped ever upward. April reeled out the string with an expert flick of her wrist. It bobbed high overhead with a jaunty dance and they came to a halt, breathless with laughter.

'That's how life should be,' he said. 'Like the flight of a kite, with the freedom to swoop and soar at will.'

'Only it isn't at will, is it?' she returned. 'It's

at the whim of the wind or the person who pulls the string.'

'So you think it's better to be in a cage of your own making?'

'Yes. At least that way you can minimise the risk of plummeting down to your destruction, or getting tangled in a tree, or quite simply being abandoned by the string-puller.'

'Or you can learn to ride the wind to the best of your ability and live your life with all the highs and the lows.'

April sighed. 'OK. We're not really talking about the kite any more, are we?'

'No. We're talking about *you*. You say you want your life to remain as it is, but that way you shut out the possibility of so much—so many opportunities. The chance to write more serious articles, the chance to change other people's lives, perhaps the chance to love and have a family.'

'I told you. I don't want that. You of all people should understand that. You've ruled it out for yourself.'

'That's different. You did want it once, or you would never have married Dean in the first place. You did believe in love and happy-ever-after, and

I don't want one man to ruin that dream for you. I don't want you to be caged in by his actions, to give up on the future you deserve.'

'I appreciate that. I do. But that happy-ever-after—it's not for me.'

'I'm sorry, April. I shouldn't have said anything. I don't want to ruin the day.' He could see sadness in her green eyes, an ache that made him want to hold her in his arms and somehow make the pain go away.

'You haven't ruined it. Not at all.'

Green eyes wide, she edged closer to him, frowned and then swiftly tied the kite string to the branch of a small sapling. Facing him, her head tipped up to meet his gaze full-on, she placed her hands on his shoulders.

'I promise. It's been an incredible day, Marcus, and one I will always remember.'

Standing on tiptoe, she kissed his cheek. A tendril of her hair whispered against his cheek, her scent tilted his senses—and he couldn't help himself. Gently he cupped her jaw and lowered his lips over hers in a kiss so sweetly sensual his head spun in sheer giddiness.

He didn't know how long they stood there, lips

locked in the flower-strewn meadow, surrounded by the gentle balm of the breeze and the gentle call of the birds, the kite still dancing above them in the cerulean sky. But finally she broke away.

'The perfect end to a perfect day,' she said, with a smile that caught at his chest.

April paced the lounge, unable to sleep, unable to do anything. That kiss *had* been the perfect end to a perfect day. But now the day was over and night had fallen and soon—oh-so-soon—she would know the answer to the question that had pounded her brain for days. The darkness outside, the deep midnight-black sky with its twinkle of stars did nothing to soothe her.

How she wished she could stare at those stars and they could tell her the future.

The click of the door alerted her and she turned to see Marcus silhouetted in the doorway.

'Sorry, I didn't want to wake you. That's why I came in here. To pace.'

'I wasn't asleep; the waiting is getting to me too.'

He came to stand beside her, by the enormous bay window.

April hesitated. 'I bought a pregnancy test. One you can do early.'

'How early?'

'I could do it now. I'm just too chicken.'

'I think you should do it. We need to know—one way or the other it's always better to know.'

He was right: better to face up to the truth rather than hide away from it. She *knew* that. Yet cold panic cascaded in a clammy sheen over her skin as she faltered out, 'OK…'

She took in a deep breath, needing to tell him something.

'But first… If I am pregnant, and if you still want custody when the baby is born, you can have it.'

She had come to realise that in this case she could trust her judgement. Marcus was not like Dean. He was a truly good man—a man with flaws, for sure, but his flaws would never permit him to hurt or demean anyone else. He could admit it when he was wrong, he could be strong, and he could be gentle. She knew with all her heart that he would keep their baby safe.

His face was pale in the light that suddenly

flooded the room as the moon pulled out from behind a cloud.

'I… Thank you, April. I swear I will be the best dad I can be.' He tried a smile. 'Now, why don't you go off and then we'll find out whether there will be any need for me to be one?'

'Wish me luck.'

With a ghost of a smile she headed for the bathroom, her heart slamming her ribcage in panic-stricken beats.

The agonising wait seemed eternal, but once the time was up April hesitated, unable to look. The tension was so taut in her tummy that she thought she might buckle with cramp.

Come on, April.

She had to know. She couldn't skulk in Marcus's bathroom for ever. It wouldn't be practical.

And so, with a near-hysterical deep breath, she looked.

CHAPTER FOURTEEN

MARCUS WAS STANDING by the window when she returned to the lounge. The light was still off, the room lit only by the pale moonbeams and star-glow from without. He spun round as she entered, his hands clenched into fists by his sides, the question in his eyes almost anguished.

'I'm not pregnant.'

She said the words clearly, woodenly, her emotions numbed, but not so frozen that she didn't see it—disappointment, zigzagging over his expression in a flash, before he stepped forward with a smile that didn't reach his eyes.

'That's a relief.'

But he couldn't pull it off.

'You don't mean that,' she said, her voice half-question, half-statement.

Three strides took him to the drinks cabinet in the corner of the room, where he pulled out a whisky bottle.

'You're right. I don't mean it.' He gestured at the bottle. 'Drink?'

'No, thank you. I don't understand. Why aren't you relieved?'

'I don't know.' He sank onto the state-of-the-art sofa, drink in hand. 'I guess this was my shot. My one chance to be a dad.' He shook his head as if in disbelief at his own words.

'It doesn't have to be. If you want a child you could adopt.'

'No. I've told you already that wouldn't be fair. There are plenty of couples like Louise and Bill out there, who can offer a child way more than I can. It would be selfish of me, unfair to them and to any child to take one. What I had to offer *this* baby was my blood; he or she would have been a baby I could have felt would be better off with me.'

'You have plenty to offer. You will be a wonderful dad. I can see that from the way you are with Charlie, the way you are with Gemma and Blake and Mia. I can see it, full-stop. More than that, you told me not to limit myself—neither should you. Try to meet a woman. Maybe the next time you opt for "physical gratification", don't walk away. Try a date instead. Give it a shot.'

Yet even as she said it emotion squeezed her gut at the idea of Marcus with another woman—Marcus holding another woman's baby.

'I can't.'

'Why not?'

'Because I'm not cut out to be a family man.'

Bitterness infused his tone as he placed the crystal tumbler on the table with a *thunk*.

'I told you my parents died—I didn't tell you how. They died in a fire. They got high and must have decided to light candles, or cook something. I woke up to the smell of smoke. I rushed to find Elvira but she wasn't there. My parents must have taken her out of her cot. I legged it into the lounge. The flames were awful. I found Elvira but I couldn't wake my parents up. I got Elvira out and then... I didn't go back in. Our neighbours held me back, said it was too dangerous.'

April released the breath she hadn't even realised she held. 'Then you *couldn't* have gone back in.'

He picked the glass up, cradled it in one hand. 'That's a matter of opinion. Maybe I could have fought harder—maybe I *should* have fought harder. Nothing would have stopped me going back in if Elvira had still been in there. I hesitated for just a minute, and in that minute the roof caved in.'

'Where were the emergency services?'

'On their way. They were too late.'

April didn't know what else to say. She could picture the scene in vivid detail: the choking, gagging fog of smoke, the intensity of heat from the red-orange flames shooting up into the dark Lycander sky…the same sky she could see right now. And the twelve-year-old boy watching, knowing that inside the building his parents lay, unable to help themselves.

'You *cannot* blame yourself.'

'Who would you suggest I blame?'

'Anyone but yourself. What happened was a tragedy, but it was brought about by a chain of circumstances and choices that were not your fault.'

'*One* of those choices was mine.'

'You didn't make a choice—you hesitated for a moment. That is not the same thing at all. Plus, your neighbours were right—you might well have died if you'd gone in.'

He raised a hand. 'Enough. I appreciate you're trying to make me feel better, but you can't. That moment of hesitation changed everything, and whilst I can't go back and change it I can at least learn from it.'

But what had he learnt? Not to love or be loved. No wonder he had never been able to let Louise and Bill in. She could only imagine the immense guilt he must feel about accepting love from a different set of parents.

No wonder he felt he was unworthy of love— he believed he had contributed to his parents' death. Just as *she* believed she had contributed to Edward's. So if she couldn't make him feel better, perhaps she could at least let him know she understood.

'You're right. I can't make you feel better. But I do understand.'

She moved closer to the sofa, wanting him to see her face.

'There's something I haven't told you. Dean and I had a baby. A little boy called Edward.'

His hand jerked and whisky slopped over the

side of the glass he had picked up once again. He deposited it on a table as he rose to stand beside her.

But she stepped away.

'Don't—please. I don't want to break down. I just want to say it. I told you about the disaster that was my marriage…how Dean made me feel like nothing. But somewhere, somehow I found the courage to leave him. I had it all planned. But the plans went wrong. Because, you see, I made a stupid decision—tried to be too clever. I should have walked straight out. Instead I decided to pack. Dean found me, guessed what I intended and went nuts. Snatched Edward. I couldn't stop him. He swatted me aside as though I truly was nothing. He ran off with our son, put him in the car and drove off. He'd been drinking, he didn't secure Edward properly, and there was a storm— rain pouring down, visibility atrocious. There was an accident and they both died.'

Marcus opened his mouth but she shook her head.

'There is nothing you can say. Nothing anyone can say. When I lost Edward I lost everything. I fell apart, sank into a pit of despair. The only reason I climbed out was because of my family—they cared for me, looked after me, and I pulled myself out, created a new life for myself. A life that I can manage. A cage, if you like, but it's better than the pit. I still know how it feels to look back and see that line in the sand—the before and after, the moment when if you could go back you could change history.'

Now he stepped forward and took her in his arms, held her tight, so close that she could feel the strength of his compassion, his sympathy, his empathy, the extent of how much he cared. She wrapped her arms around him and returned the pressure.

When he spoke it was over her head, his voice raw with emotion. 'I wish with all my heart that I could turn back the clock for you—that I could somehow protect you from the loss and pain you have endured.'

'Thank you.'

Eventually they pulled apart and he looked at her, his dark eyes intense. 'Stay,' he said, the one word filled with meaning.

'I don't understand.'

'In the meadow I asked you to stay in Lycander. I'm asking again. Stay. Here. With me. For a week, a month, a few days.'

For a stupid, wonderful instant she wanted to say yes, to stay for a while—but then she shook her head. 'It wouldn't work. Right now you're feeling sorry for me, and that is no basis for any sort of relationship.'

'This isn't to do with pity.'

'Then what *is* it to do with?'

'I want to spend more time with you. Isn't that what you suggested I do? Go on a date? Try for more than short-term physical gratification?'

'I did. But not with me.' Tears prickled the back of her eyes and she blinked hard, refusing to allow them exit.

He reached out and took both her hands in his, his grasp gentle and yet full of strength and re-assurance. '*Yes*, with you,' he said. 'Why don't we spend some time together because we *want* to? See where it could go. No expectations, no promises...'

'I can't do that.' The very idea caused panic, a visceral fear, to judder through her. 'And you deserve a woman who can—a woman there's the possibility of a future with. I have nothing left to give. I can only maintain my cage—my insulated bubble, as I prefer to think of it. These past weeks I've ventured out—with you. I've had a taste of the world outside my bubble. I've experienced joy and happiness and anger, and I've witnessed pain and suffering. Now I need to go back into my bubble.'

Hurt flashed across his face, followed by acceptance, and in that instant she knew exactly what he was thinking. That he wasn't enough—wasn't enough to make her want to stay out of her cage. That what he had to offer was insufficient.

'It's not you.' How could she make those clichéd words real? 'Don't you see? I can't do it. It's too much, too scary.' And he deserved so much more than her.

'It's OK.'

His deep voice soothed her.

'I understand—and you're right. It was a stupid idea. Not because of you, but because of me. I hope that one day someone will come along and entice you out of that bubble.'

Helplessness assailed her, along with an absurd desire either to pummel his chest with her fists or throw herself against him and burst into tears.

Could she agree? Could she stay with him? See what happened?

No. Because she knew what would happen. She would fall for him...plummet into an abyss of emotion that she could not deal with. So all she could do was get out. But the thought of leaving—right here and now like this, when they had both shared so much—seemed impossible. Seemed wrong.

'That won't happen,' she heard herself say. 'But I hope that one day *you* will find happiness and love and have the chance to be a dad. I know you'll make a great one.'

And still she couldn't bring herself to leave... couldn't pull her hands from his. Realisation hit her like lead. It was too late—she had already fallen. She loved him, and was already mid-tumble into a mire of sensation and feelings.

No. She punched the knowledge aside in sheer repudiation. This wasn't love—it was confusion...a need to say goodbye properly.

She looked up at him. 'Marcus?'

The word was half-question, half-entreaty.

'Could we...could we have one more night?'

There was no need for further words. He pulled

her into his arms and relief, gratitude and desire enmeshed her. A small moan escaped her lips, and then all else was forgotten in their bitter-sweet embrace as he swept her up into his arms and carried her from the room.

Marcus opened his eyes and knew that April was gone. His whole being was bereft, even as he felt some grim satisfaction that he had kept the promise she had extracted from him in the early hours of the morning.

'Please let me say goodbye now.'

Her hair had been tickling his chin and his arms had been wrapped around her. He hadn't wanted her to say goodbye at all. But he'd respected her wishes and agreed.

Of course he'd known when she'd woken—had forced himself to remain still as she'd slipped from the bed, quietly picked up her clothes and dropped a feather-light kiss on his cheek before she'd tiptoed out of the room. And out of his life. Because shortly after that he'd heard the door click shut and had known that April was gone.

He needed to get on with his life—there could have been no future with April. He had been a fool even to contemplate any deviation from his path.

April had been through so much—had worked out a way to live her life despite the tragedy she had experienced. He could offer her nothing, really, except perhaps medium-term gratification. For a mad moment he'd been allowed a glimpse of a different future—had had a vision of himself as a dad—but he knew now it had been nothing but an illusion. April had been sensible enough to see that and to reject the insubstantial offer he had made her.

He closed his eyes and allowed himself the memory of the past few hours—hours of such bittersweet joy that his gut wrenched at the knowledge they would never be repeated. He'd never hold April in his arms again, never caress her skin, hear her laugh or...

Enough.

He'd survived for years without April and he'd survive now. There was work to be done and plenty of it.

Swinging himself out of bed, he headed for the bathroom, closing his senses to the elusive drift of April's perfume—the delicate rose that hitched his breath in his chest. Avoiding the kitchen, he left the house as soon as possible.

Yet everywhere seemed to hold a memory, and by evening his head pounded with the effort of not thinking.

A knock on the office door elicited a sigh and a terse, 'Come in.' Surprise raised his brows as Louise entered, a tentative smile on her face. He couldn't remember either Louise or Bill ever coming to his office without prior arrangement.

Maybe because you made it plain they weren't welcome.

He could almost hear April's voice and now infused his own with defensive cheer. 'Louise! How lovely to see you. I was going to call later to thank you and Bill for everything you've done. Sunita said you've been fantastic in the nursery.'

'I was glad to help. Those poor parents needed somewhere they knew their children would be safe and fed and looked after whilst they tried to put their lives back together. But that's not why I'm here. I got a thank-you message from April, but I understand that she has now left Lycander?'

'Yes.'

'I'm sorry. I saw the way you looked at each

other last week and I thought… I hoped that maybe you two were together.'

'No.'

'Do you have feelings for her?'

Marcus blinked at her, feeling a touch flummoxed. He and Louise quite simply did not have conversations like this.

'I…'

Louise continued almost chattily. 'I think you do. Maybe you even love her.'

The words seemed to come from a long way away, and then they exploded in a sonic boom around him. *Love.* He *loved* April. The idea was so ginormous, so huge, so terrifying he couldn't even summon the ability to deny it.

'I…it doesn't matter if I do. I asked her to stay and she didn't.'

Louise looked at him as if he were missing a few brain cells. 'Did you tell her how you feel or did you just let her go?'

'I let her go. You can't *make* people love you.'

'No, you can't. But you *can* try to persuade them. I know I'm biased, but what's not to love? You are kind, generous, strong, brave and loyal.'

His body flinched in automatic rejection of the

words and Louise leant forward, placed her hands on his desk.

'Marcus. There are things that I should have said before. Things I didn't say because you never wished to speak of them and I thought it best not to. Perhaps I was simply too much of a coward. That fire was not your fault and neither was the death of your parents. It was a tragedy brought about by the choices your parents made. The choices you have made in *your* life have been principled and honourable. You were twelve years old but you saved Elvira—at great risk to yourself.'

'But I didn't save *them*.'

'No. You didn't. And no one expected you to. You would have died if you had gone back into that building and that would have been an even bigger tragedy. You are a *good* person, Marcus, and I am proud that you are my son. Now believe in yourself. If you love April tell her so. Don't leave it too late, like I have with you.'

'It's not too late.'

Marcus moved around the desk and without thought took this wonderful woman into his arms. 'I love you too, and when I get back we'll talk. You and me and Dad.'

'It's a deal.' Louise made a shooing motion. 'Now, *go*.'

And with that she left.

Before he could even begin to think about their conversation there was another knock on the door and Frederick entered.

Marcus rose to his feet.

'I have come to grant you leave of absence so you can go and find April,' said Frederick.

Marcus blinked. 'I wasn't aware I'd taken out a social media advert proclaiming my emotional state.'

'I am not an idiot. Plus I recognise the signs. It's not so long ago that you told me to go after the woman I loved. I am here to return the favour. Go. But before you do—your father is waiting to see you.'

Marcus guessed he shouldn't be surprised.

Frederick left and Bill entered, for all the world as if this were some Broadway show: *Exit the Prince, stage left. Enter the father, stage right.*

Stepping forward he shook hands with Bill, who looked at him apologetically.

'I know Louise has just been here, but I wanted to wish you luck and echo what she said. I'm proud of you, and I couldn't have wished for a better son.' His adoptive dad grinned slightly awkwardly. 'And I hope we can spend a bit more time together in the future.'

'I'd like that.' And he meant every word.

Bill held out a hand. 'Good luck with April. Take a tip from me and don't give up. I didn't have it easy with Louise, you know. She had some damn fool idea in her head that because she couldn't have kids I wouldn't want her. I told her that all I wanted in the world was her, and it was true. And then we were blessed with you and Elvira, so we did good. So will you.'

If only it could be that easy. He knew everyone meant well, but they seemed to believe that April would just fall into his arms, and Marcus knew damn well that it wouldn't be that simple. The odds of her loving him back seemed remote. Perhaps she would elect to keep walking away and not look back.

His stomach clenched and then he thumped the desk. *No.* He would not think like that. He was a fighter and, so help him, he would fight for April like he had never fought before.

* * *

April stared out of the window at the London drizzle. It suited her mood—grey, miserable, dull—and she was missing Marcus with an ache she didn't want to acknowledge. Her desolation was deep, poignant…as though a part of her was missing.

And it wasn't only Marcus—she missed Lycander, the community centre, the people, even Roberto the chauffeur, whom she had bonded with over their mutual love of chocolate.

She gave another sigh—one she tried to swallow as her father walked in. She summoned a smile, though from Alex Fotherington's expression he wasn't fooled for an instant.

'Come on, petal. Why don't you tell me what's wrong?'

'Me. I'm just all *wrong*—befuddled and confused and—'

'I'm glad.'

April stared at him. 'Glad? Well, gee, thanks a bunch, Dad.'

'I *am* glad. Because you're feeling *something*.'

'I don't *want* to feel anything.' Talk about throwing her toys out of the pram… 'Last time I felt miserable it was—'

'Was over a tragedy you could have done nothing about. That was flat-out misery of the type I hope you never have to feel again. This is a different misery, and I suspect it's one you can choose to do something about.'

'How?'

'I think you've woken up, and I think all the emotions you've kept caged are surfacing and you're starting to live life again. I'd further guess that your befuddled confusion has something to do with love. If it does, don't reject it, April. Love is too precious.'

Love? The word rebounded around the room like a cannonball and she could feel the reverberations through her whole body She *loved* Marcus! What an idiot she was. A fool thrice over.

'I *have* to reject it!' she yelled suddenly, aghast with herself at the volume of her voice. 'Look where love landed me last time.'

'"Last time" was a long time ago, and a lot of people were taken in by Dean. But Dean was *one* person. You made *one* mistake in love.'

'And it cost my son his *life*.'

'No, sweetheart. Your belief in love did *not* cost Edward his life. Dean's actions and some very bad luck cost Edward his life, and that does not mean you should never love or trust again. I don't believe you ever loved Dean. You were young and you got carried away. If life had worked out I think you would have realised that mistake without the tragedy that unfolded. Love did not cost Edward his life—love made the short time he had on this earth a happy time. Love is a precious commodity, and if you're lucky enough to love and be loved I hope you embrace it rather than shut it out.'

April stared at her dad's much-loved face and then rose to her feet and hugged him. 'Thank you. I still feel befuddled and confused, but I also feel better.'

'You're very welcome, sweetheart. I wish you luck with your decision.'

April sank down by the window again and wondered what to do...

Two days later

April sat by the graveside, ran her fingers over the headstone. She touched the items she'd placed so lovingly around the site. The windmill that turned in the breeze—Edward had been fascinated by the whirr and swirl of the colours as a baby. A tall vase filled with bright flowers—a standing order with the local florist still honoured. Edward's headstone.

She wasn't sure how long she'd been sitting there, gazing at the stone.

'Edward, I love you, oh-so-much, and I am so very sorry I couldn't protect you.'

Hugging her knees, she looked out over the cemetery and thought about her chosen course of action. And although there was panic in the mix of her feelings, there was also a sense of rightness. She did love Marcus, and—

She tensed at the sound of approaching footsteps, praying it wasn't a member of Dean's family...

She rose, turned, and froze in disbelief, sure she must be in the grip of hallucination. But there was something too real about the solid bulk, the aura, the pent-up energy of Marcus Alrikson that brooked no denial.

'I'm sorry to come here...to intrude...but I didn't want to risk the chance of missing you. Would you prefer it if I wait somewhere else? Or we could arrange to meet later? Or—?'

'No.' She shook her head. 'I'm glad you're here. It sounds a little nuts, but I came here to tell Edward something important—to clear my head and make my peace… I'm not sure—' She broke off, aware that she wasn't making sense. 'How did you find me?' The question was more curious than angry.

'Your parents told me where you were.'

'They did?'

'I persuaded them that it was a desperate case.'

A horrible thought entered her head. 'If it's about the article, I'll send you a copy to approve first—'

'The article? Of *course* it's not about the article. You can write what you like. Hell, I'll pose for a centrefold in a pair of tightie-whities, if you like.'

April stared at him. He sounded…agitated. Marcus Alrikson? Agitated?

Suddenly, to her own surprise, she laughed, knowing that if Edward's spirit could hear he wouldn't mind.

'That won't be necessary. So what's so desperate?' A sudden lurch of hope jumped around in her tummy.

'I should never have kept that promise,' he said. 'To let you say goodbye. Because I don't want you to walk away. Not then, not now, not ever.'

'Why not?' The words were a whisper.

'Because I love you.'

There was a silence and then he smiled, as if by saying the words he had released magic into the air. And perhaps he had, because tendrils of potential happiness seemed to be unfurling inside her.

Yet how could this be possible?

She shook her head. 'It doesn't make sense. You said yourself that you didn't want love, or a relationship—that you *couldn't* love.'

'That is what I thought. What I have believed for too many years. It took you to show me that I was wrong. On all counts. You see, I grew up with no understanding of what real love meant. Until Elvira was born. When my parents brought her home I knew that I would do anything for her. But then the fire happened and something inside me froze. I still loved Elvira—but I couldn't love anyone else. Couldn't acknowledge love because I was so mixed up. But somehow you melted that freeze. Over the past weeks you've changed me, unlocked something inside me. You made me want to reach out—made me question my perspective on the past and my upbringing. But most of all you made me love you. I accept that this may all be too much, that you don't love *me*, but I want a chance to persuade you to do just that.'

April smiled suddenly as she reached down for her bag. 'Look.' She delved inside and pulled out an envelope, handed it to him. 'Open it.'

He did so. 'A ticket to Lycander? You were coming back?'

'Yes. To find you. To tell you that I love you. That I have fallen for you hook, line and sinker. That I can't go back into my insulated bubble, my cage, and I don't want to. I'd prefer to be free to love you, because love is too precious to waste. I *love* you, Marcus. I love your honour and your integrity. I love the way you make me feel—the way you have pulled me back into the sunshine. I love that you make me feel safe and exasperated and downright annoyed. I love how much you care about people and making the world a better place. I love you. And I want to spend all my days and nights with you.'

His smile lit his face, lit her world, made her glow inside and out.

'There's something else as well. I still haven't got my period. I don't know what, if anything, that means. I still might not be pregnant, given the test we did was negative, but it's made me think. Either way, I would love to have a baby with you. I know it will be an emotional journey, but...'

With Marcus by her side it was a journey she knew she could take—one she wanted to take.

'Edward will always have a place in my heart, but my love for him is different from the love I will have for another baby.'

'And because of my love for you Edward will always have a place in *my* heart too.'

She heard the sincerity in his voice, knew that he meant every word, and stepped forward into the warmth of his embrace, resting her head on his chest and knowing with all her heart that this man was her soul mate.

'You opened my eyes, April. To the possibility of a future I thought I could never have. A future filled with love and happiness.'

She smiled up at him, secure in the knowledge that it was a future they would walk into together, with no regrets at all.

EPILOGUE

Ten months later

APRIL LOOKED UP as her husband—her *husband…* the word still filled her with love, awe and a near-disbelief at her own luck that this wonderful man loved her—entered the room on tiptoe.

'She's asleep,' April whispered as Marcus approached the cot where their beautiful daughter Eleanor lay, her tiny hands curled into fists by her head, which was covered with wisps of dark curls.

'Nearly as beautiful as her mother,' Marcus said, and April grinned up at him.

'Very diplomatic—but I know perfectly well that this little one already has you twisted round her little finger.' She gazed tenderly down at her daughter. 'And I don't blame you one little bit. I still can't believe how blessed we are.'

It was true—from the moment they had discovered that she was, in fact, pregnant Marcus had been her rock. His joy and his pride and his understanding had been further proof, if she had needed it, that this man was truly amazing.

The past months had been a wonderful journey they had made together. Each day had cemented their love further, laid down a foundation she knew would endure for the rest of their lives. Together they had chosen and bought a beautiful house in Lycander; together they had prepared a nursery for their baby—painted the walls, stencilled drawings in their spare time.

April continued to work at the community centre, and had written a series of articles on the plight of the poor and disadvantaged in Lycander, and Marcus continued to help forge change in the country he loved. And through it all their love for each other and their unborn baby had grown.

Of course there had been difficult moments—moments when poignant memories of Edward had caused her sadness—but always Marcus had been there, with his love, and together they had created new and happy memories in the present.

'I know. We are truly blessed. I have no idea what I did to deserve this much happiness.'

Marcus put his arm around her, held her close,

and she felt his love as warm as a blanket surrounding her.

'I love you, April. Now and for ever.'

'Now and for ever,' she echoed, meaning it with every fibre of her body and soul.

* * * * *

B